The Adventures of Pilla the Pup and Other Stories

The Adventures of Pilla the Pup and Other Stories

Uma Anand

Illustrations By Mario Miranda

An imprint of Om Books International

Published in 2015 by

An imprint of Om Books International

Corporate & Editorial Office
A 12, Sector 64, Noida 201 301
Uttar Pradesh, India
Phone: +91 120 477 4100
Email: editorial@ombooks.com
Website: www.ombooksinternational.com

Sales Office
107, Ansari Road, Darya Ganj
New Delhi 110 002, India
Phone: +91 11 2326 3363, 2326 5303, 4000 9000
Fax: +91 11 2327 8091
Email: sales@ombooks.com
Website: www.ombooks.com

ISBN: 978-93-84225-30-8

Printed in India

10 9 8 7 6 5 4 3 2 1

Contents

The Tale Of Lumbdoom The Long-tailed Langur

Dul Dul

The Magic Clay Horse

For
My nieces Yamina, Raheela and Fatima

1

Dul Dul: The Magic Clay Horse

Poor old Sonoo, the grey-bearded Potter, was having a dreadful time. All day he had been trying to make a simple clay pot. Try as he might, however, his hand would slip, or the clay would suddenly plop off the wheel, as though it had a will of its own. Once the pot was almost ready, and Sonoo was just about to remove it from the whirling wheel, when pop, pop! right out of the centre of the little pot blew two big, fat bubbles. Up, up, they came and then, naughtily, burst right in the old man's face, as though to mock him. The pot was spoilt again.

"Oh dear!" sighed the potter. "Whatever shall I do? It's midday now, and not a pot made. No supper for me if I cannot make and sell a pot today. Drat this clay! There must be an imp in it!"

So saying, Sonoo took a very large lump of clay and struck it on the wheel. He gave the wheel a sharp twirl.

"Shape yourself silly," he cried angrily.

The wheel whirred; the clay grew long and fat, wide and thin. The potter looked and stared, and then gave a loud gasp! For, there before his eyes, the clay had shaped itself into the oddest, fattest, naughtiest little horse that ever snorted!

"Hee! Hee!" neighed the little horse wobbling off the Potter's wheel, "Ha! Ha! Hee! Hee!" and, his wet podgy feet leaving big sloshy marks all over the floor, the horse wobbled shakily towards the gate.

"Hey little fellow," cried the amazed potter, "you come back here. Don't you forget you belong to me."

"Hee! Hee!" mocked the little horse, not bothering to turn round, "Ha! Ha!"

And off he went.

Off trotted Dul Dul. Out of the gate and on to the street.

As he turned a corner, he heard a snuffle and a yap, and came face-to-face with the smallest, fluffiest pup, with the curliest tail you ever saw!

"Yap, yap," barked the puppy.

"Hee! Hee!" neighed Dul Dul. Who are you?

"I'm Pilla the Pup," said the curly-tailed puppy. "Are you coming to live on our street?"

"Oh no, I'm off to see the big, wide world. I'm Dul Dul, the Magic Clay Horse," Dul Dul replied, very proudly indeed.

"Oh Dul Dul, please take me with you," begged Pilla.

"Well, then we must make friends," said Dul Dul. "Hullo Pilla," and he bowed very properly.

Pilla was most excited and happy. "Oh thank you, Dul Dul" he cried, and bounced forward trying to bow like Dul Dul.

And what do you think happened? Pilla bumped his nose into Dul Dul's. It went right into the wet clay and stuck fast!

Oh, how funny they looked! But Dul Dul was cross, and Pilla was frightened.

Lots of people gathered round and laughed at them.

"Come on, have a tug-of-war," they shouted. "One! Two! Three!"

Pilla tugged. Dul Dul tugged. Pop! Back they fell, both of them. Pilla ran off yelping. Dul Dul plonked into a basket full of tiny new potatoes.

"Oh bother!" he cried. "Now what shall I do for the big dip in my nose?"

Dul Dul picked himself out of the basket of new potatoes, feeling sad about the dip in his nice nose. Then he had a bright idea! He pressed his nose against a small round potato, and it snugly fitted into the dent! Feeling very happy, Dul Dul trotted off once more.

He soon saw a white gate that opened into a lovely garden. It was a hot day, and Dul Dul was hungry. He thought he would rest under a big shady tree, and crop the fresh, green grass.

He found a spreading banyan, that looked to him like a whole forest in itself. It had so many trunks and swinging roots. The grass under it was thick and juicy. Dul Dul was soon busy eating.

All at once there was a flap flap flapping noise, and a harsh mocking cry.

"Kaa-Kaa-Kaa, look at this funny fellow! Kaa-Kaa-Kaa," and a big black crow flew down, and began pecking at the little potato in Dul Dul's nose.

In a second, dozens of crows came down, "Kaa-Kaa-Kaa," they cawed, "drive him out of our banyan-home."

Poor Dul Dul, he put his head down, and kicked his back legs. He swished his tail, he flicked his ears. But there was little he could do against naughty Kaa and his friends. At last, frightened and bruised he ran into a hollow at the base of the big tree trunk.

The crows soon flew off. Dul Dul sat panting, in a dark corner of the hollow, too tired and frightened to move.

2

Dul Dul's First Good Deed

Deep in the hollow of the big, old banyan tree, Dul Dul sat still. He was waiting for Kaa the Crow and his friends to fly away.

Suddenly, in the dark, he heard a soft sniffle. Someone was crying! He turned about trying to see through the gloom.

"Hullo," he whispered softly, "who is it? Who is crying?"

"M-m-mee," said a tiny squeaky voice.

"Who is me?" asked Dul Dul very puzzled! "And where are you?"

"Here," came a squeak from somewhere near Dul Dul's tail. He turned about carefully, and there he saw the smallest baby squirrel in the world.

"You sweet little chap," said Dul Dul, quite forgetting his own troubles, "why are you crying?"

"I am l-lost," sobbed the squirrel. "Mama had just brought me from our woolly nest to a hollow in a shady tree, and when she went back to fetch my sister, I tried to follow her. But I lost her, and now I am h-h-hungry."

"Oh dear!" said Dul Dul, "I wish I could give you something to eat."

Just then he had a bright idea, "Those naughty crows tried to eat the potato in my nose. Do you think you could eat it?"

He put his nose near the little squirrel.

"I will try," and so saying, the small, furry creature began to nibble delicately at the potato.

"I hope I do not get a tummy ache," he giggled.

Dul Dul laughed. The nibbling tickled him a bit. Also he felt happy, having found a friend.

The little squirrel was busy eating, and as he ate, Dul Dul began telling him all about himself. His voice

sounded very funny because sometimes the nibbling made it come out of his nose.

"I am really a magic horse," he told his new friend, "and I made myself on old Sonoo the potter's wheel. You should have seen his face when I ran away from him! But I should have let him bake me in his oven, as my clay is not yet hard. That is how Pilla the Pup's nose got stuck in mine. And that is also why I had to put the potato in, to hide the dip. First I was cross about it. But just as well I did, as now you have been able to have a jolly good feed. I must say I did not like it when that nasty crow, I think his name is Kaa, and all his friends pecked at it. I think Kaa is a big bully!"

And he told the squirrel all about Kaa.

"Wait," said the squirrel, quite perky after his meal. "I'll peep out, and see if they have gone."

So, very softly he crept up to the mouth of the hollow.

The little squirrel peeped round the corner of the hollow. Not a sound could be heard, the crow, and all his friends had flown away.

The squirrel nodded to Dul Dul over his shoulder, "Come on, all's well, friend," he squeaked.

They came out, and the breeze was cool and fresh. It made them feel happy.

"Hey catch me," cried the squirrel as he went.

Dul Dul ran after him. The squirrel was very quick. He ran round in circles, and while he was trying to run about, he got behind him, ran up his legs, and on to his back!

"Hee! Hee!" giggled Dul Dul, "you are tickling my neck!"

"Gee-up Pony!" cried the squirrel.

"My name is Dul Dul. I am a magic clay horse," shouted Dul Dul.

"Well, I am Pitki," the squirrel replied. "Do take me for a ride, Dul Dul."

So Dul Dul galloped off with Pitki on his back.

He ran and ran, right to the other end of the park. Suddenly he came to the edge of a big blue lily pond. He stopped, just in time, at the brink of the pool. Pitki, who was having a grand ride, and not holding on to Dul Dul, got a jerk. He gave a squeak, and before you could blink an eye, he flew over Dul Dul's head, right into the middle of the pond!

Dul Dul gave a gasp, "Oh Pitki, I am sorry," he cried. "Wait, I am coming to help you."

Pitki, who had gone right over Dul Dul's head, plop into the lily pool, soon found himself sinking down, down, down. The water got into his ears and nose. Oh! It was a horrid feeling.

At the bottom of the lily pool, Pitki, whose eyes were closed, and who could not have helped it in any case, went bump into the head of a fat green bullfrog. The bullfrog was diving in to catch a water grub, and he got bumped by a soggy, wet "thing". He caught the "thing" in his large, ugly mouth. It felt woolly and not at all like a "thing" that a bullfrog could eat!

Now, Dul Dul, who had so bravely told Pitki he would help him, put one hoof into the pool. Oof!

It was WET! He quickly took it out. "What if I melt in the water?" he thought. "Then both Pitki and I will die. I must try and help in some other way."

No one was there to tell him what to do, and he also felt bad for not being brave enough to die for his friend. So, closing his eyes, and taking a deep breath he was about to leap into the pool when, with a swoosh, out popped the bullfrog with a big splash! He sat on a lily pad with Pitki drooping from his huge ugly mouth.

"Oh please ... oh thank you ... oh goody-good," cried Dul Dul getting all mixed up. He was so happy.

Dul Dul grew quieter.

"May I have my friend?" he asked politely.

"Gawk! And whap bhill you gib me instead?" asked the bullfrog, who could not speak clearly because his mouth was full of squirrel.

"Oh let me think," said poor Dul Dul.

"Thing fazd," croaked the bullfrog, rolling his eyes.

Dul Dul did not know what the bullfrog would like in exchange for Pitki. But he was ready to do anything to get his friend back. So he said very politely, "Would you like to have the rest of the potato I have in the dip in my nose? Pitki ate most of it, but ..."

He had not even finished his polite speech when the bullfrog who was a very bad tempered fellow and always shouting at those who looked smaller than himself, croaked out, "Bodado! Goo-awk. Mud in your eye!"

This rude remark made Dul Dul very angry. So he turned around, and kicked his hind legs up throwing a big shower of slushy mud into the bullfrog's eyes!

"Goo-awk! Gawk!" gasped the big bully. And he opened his mouth to gulp some air. Out dropped Pitki, on to the lily pad, near the frog's feet.

Without thinking of himself, Dul Dul jumped into the pool. He was up to his knees in water. But he was no longer afraid of getting wet.

The bullfrog saw Dul Dul coming towards him. He thought Dul Dul might catch hold of him and crush him under his hoofs. So, like most big bullies, he did not wait to find out, but with a loud croak, dived into the pool.

Dul Dul was glad to see him go. Because, to tell the truth, he was not at all sure he could manage to rescue Pitki as well as fight the frog at the same time.

He picked Pitki up gently in his mouth, and took him back to the bank. There he laid his friend down on the grass, and rubbed him all over with his muzzle. Pitki woke up.

"Where am I?" he asked faintly.

3

Pitki Gets Into More Trouble

Dul Dul was happy. He now knew his little friend would live. He threw his head up, and neighed loudly, "Hee-hee Hee-hee!" in sheer joy. He kicked up his legs, and capered round the squirrel.

"Come on, Pitki," he called to his friend, "let's be off on our travels."

"Dul Dul," called Pitki weakly, "please stop jumping about. It makes me dizzy. You will have to help me up."

"Oh Pitki, I am sorry. How silly of me not to have thought of you. Are you feeling better now?" asked Dul Dul, very ashamed of his selfish wish to be off soon. "Wait, I will kneel down, you can scramble onto my back."

Before Dul Dul could help Pitki up, a dreadful thing happened. Pitki was still lying flat on his back, all wet and limp, looking more dead than alive. Dul Dul had come up to him, when he heard a shrill cry, and a great flutter of wings. A swift, shadow-like form dived from the sky, past his ears, and to his horror he saw a huge, swooping hawk lift little Pitki in his talons, and streak away with him, to the top of the tallest tree.

It all happened so quickly, that poor Pitki did not even have time to cry out.

"Oh Pitki," wailed Dul Dul, "whatever shall I do for you now?"

And he was so sad, he put his head down on the ground and sobbed bitterly.

While Dul Dul hid his face in the grass, and cried over his poor little friend's fate, Pitki, tightly held in the claws of the hawk, went sailing up, up, right into the blue sky. He would have enjoyed this wonderful flight if only he were not in for such a horrid end! He felt sure the hawk would soon gobble him up.

As the hawk flew on, Pitki saw that he was being taken to the top of a very big tree, near the Big Banyan where he had found Dul Dul. He tried to twist around in the bird's talons, but they were so tightly round him, he could hardly breathe.

The hawk was about to come down to its nest, and like an aeroplane slowly circling round the airport before landing, the hawk, too began flying slower and slower, in circles. Pitki felt its claws become a little looser. Losing no time, Pitki turned his head and nipped the hawk's leg with his sharp teeth. The hawk gave a shrill screech, but Pitki held on with all his might. Just then, another hawk swooped past, trying to knock Pitki out of his captor's claws.

The stinging pain of Pitki's little teeth, and the sudden attack from the second hawk, were too much for the big bird. Its claws opened and Pitki fell!

Down he went through a lot of rustling, green leaves; past twigs and branches, and then, just as he was getting very dizzy, he landed with a thud, in a large, soft nest!

As he lay panting but happy, he heard a small voice say, "Well, well, well, and who invited you here, pray?" But he was so giddy he could not make out a word.

He sat up, swaying dizzily, and tried a sort of smile. The small birdie, who was watching Pitki with wide eyes and an open beak, saw that he was about to fall out of the nest.

"Hey! Hold on," she tweeted, and she spread her little wings out to keep him from toppling over. Pitki gave a happy little gurgle, and curling up into a round ball in the middle of the nest, he fell fast asleep!

"Oh dear," thought the little birdie, "I wonder what Mama will say to our new guest!"

Just then Mama Bird came flying back to the nest, with a nice, fat grub for her baby chick. Now, instead of opening her beak wide and tweeting greedily for the food, as she always did, the little chick flapped her wings, nodded her head towards Pitki and kept saying, "Look! Look! Mama, look ..."

"Goodness me!" exclaimed Mama Bird, dropping the grub from her beak in surprise. "Who have we here?"

She stared closely at Pitki, and gave a whistle, "Why, I do believe it must be poor Mrs Squirrel's lost son, Pitki. You remember, Cheep Cheep, I told you about the grey squirrel family who have just moved into the hollow, in the middle of our tree?"

Cheep Cheep nodded her head very hard though she did not really remember much about it.

"Well," went on Mama, "during her house-moving she lost her naughty little son, who ran off on his own, into the big wide world. Oh dearie me! However did he come here?"

"Mama," chirped Cheep Cheep, "he fell from the sky."

"Tut! Tut! What a foolish little squirrel. Well, you just keep watch over him, and I must fly down at once to give his mother the good news. I shall bring her back with me."

Off she flew. Cheep Cheep perched on the edge of the nest and kept a close watch on the sleeping Pitki.

Mama Bird flew down to the hollow in the middle of the big tree trunk. She knocked politely on the edge of the hollow though to tell the truth, she was so excited about the wonderful news she had for Mrs Squirrel that she could barely wait.

Luckily, Mrs Squirrel was in, and peeped out calling, "Who is it?"

"Mrs Squirrel! Oh, Mrs Squirrel," flapped Mama Bird, "I have such news, you will never believe. I can hardly believe it myself ... indeed, I don't know how to..."

"Goodness, Mama Bird," cried Mrs Squirrel, who was always a little frightened of everything since the time Pitki had run away and got lost.

"What is it? Has Cheep Cheep fallen out? Oh dear! Oh please tell me, I cannot bear it!" and poor Mrs Squirrel burst into a flood of tears.

"Dear, dear, calm yourself. Do forgive me: How silly I am," chattered Mama Bird, patting her friend with a wing, and stroking her head with her beak, to calm her. "It's wonderful news. Pitki is safe and sound and ..."

"Pitki?" squeaked Mrs Squirrel, "Are you sure? How? What? Why? Oh! Oh! Oh!" And believe it or not, she was so excited and happy, she began to weep again!

"Now, now, this will never do," scolded Mama Bird, "you must not cry any more. Pitki is in my nest. How he got there, I cannot tell. Cheep Cheep says he fell from the sky!"

"I'm sorry," said Mrs Squirrel, drying her tears with, a paw, "it's just that I cannot believe my good fortune. I thought my foolish son was dead. Come, I'm quite calm now. Let us go. And, dear Mama Bird, thank you ever so ..."

"That's enough of that," broke in Mama Bird. "You just come up, and I'll fly ahead to see that all is well."

So Mrs Squirrel scurried up as fast, as she could, to her naughty son, Pitki.

4

Dul Dul Meets An Old Friend

Pitki had landed quite safe and sound in Mama Bird's
nest, but poor Dul Dul knew nothing about his lucky

escape from the hawk. He was sure he would never see his dear friend again.

So, very sadly, he started off on his way. He did not frisk or trot, nor did he answer the little birds as they greeted him with a cheery whistle. He took no notice of a pretty, purple and blue butterfly that settled for a moment on his head and asked him who he was and where he was going.

Shaking his head sadly from side to side, he plodded slowly through the forest.

A loud yapping made him turn round. From behind a prickly bush out came a frightened bunny, its ears flat against its back, followed by a puppy yelling and running as fast as it could, followed by a very angry billy goat, charging with its head down.

The bunny flashed past Dul Dul's nose; the puppy bumped into him and the billy goat dashed into both of them, and they all fell over in a heap!

The bunny, who had run past, heard the bump! Bang! Thud! He turned round. When he saw Dul Dul, the pup and the goat, all flopping about with their legs kicking, tails flicking, ears flapping, he burst out

laughing! He laughed, and laughed so much, he had to hold his tummy, while the tears ran down his face!

Dul Dul was the first to pick himself out of the muddle, and he rolled the pup over to one side. To his surprise, he found it was the same little dog he had met on the street, outside the Potter's home!

"Why, Pilla! Whatever are you up to now?" cried Dul Dul, who had really been quite cross about the dip Pilla had made in his nice clay nose, when they had first met.

"Oh Dul Dul," yapped Pilla, bouncing up and down with joy. "I am so happy to meet you again! Please save me from Garbar. He is such a cross old thing!"

"Cross old thing, am I?" said the goat, pulling his horns out of the ground where they had got stuck

when he had tumbled over. "And how would you feel, you silly pup, if someone nipped your tail while you were asleep?"

"Pilla! How naughty of you," scolded Dul Dul, trying to look very sternly at Pilla, who stopped bouncing, and sat still with his head down and his curly tail quite limp and straight behind him.

"I promise ... I cross my heart ... I hope to die ... I really truly promise you, Dul Dul, it was all a mistake!" he gabbled, getting all mixed up, and his tail curling again in his excitement. "I was looking for a bone in the hay."

"Ho! Ho! Ho!" giggled the bunny. "Old Garbar's tail is just like a bone! Ho! Ho!

"Ee-ow!" He gave a leap, as Garbar, made a sudden charge at him. In a jiffy, the bunny disappeared down a burrow nearby.

"Well, that settles him," grunted Garbar crossly. "One day he'll giggle himself into his grave. Hrrmph!" And he gave a big snort.

Dul Dul hid a smile, as he did not want to annoy Garbar any more. He went up to him, and said, very politely, "Please forgive Pilla. He didn't really mean it. I'm sure he didn't! Why, you know, he was trying to bow to me, and he bumped into my nose, and made a big dip in it. It's just that Pilla bounces so! He wriggles and jumps and can never keep still. It shakes his brains up, I think, and so he is never certain what he is doing."

Dul Dul stopped speaking, quite breathless with having made such a long speech. All three of them were quiet. Pilla was trying hard to sit still, so that his brains could settle a bit. He thought Dul Dul to be very clever indeed, to have found out why he was always getting into trouble, though he did wonder how Dul Dul knew so much about him, when they had only met once. Garbar was letting his anger cool off, and also getting back his breath. He felt quite tired after all that charging around! And Dul Dul was hoping Garbar would accept the sudden reason he had made up for Pilla's odd behaviour.

Finally, Garbar raised his head, "Oh well, let's forget it. I want a nice, cool drink. It's hot."

"I know where, I know!" yapped Pilla, up in a trice, and ready to be off again.

"Now, Pilla, do stop bouncing," said Dul Dul firmly. "Come along, Garbar. I can take you to the lily pool. But I am afraid Mr Bullfrog, who lives in it, is no friend of mine," he added.

"I'm not afraid of a silly bullfrog," snorted Garbar, "lead the way."

"Please, please, please may I come too?" pleaded Pilla.

"We-ell?" said Dul Dul looking at Garbar.

"Come along, silly," grunted Garbar gruffly, adding quickly, "but mind you, don't scamper around and get tangled up in my legs. One fall is enough for me. I'm not as young as I was."

"I promise," said Pilla, very happy to be taken with them. "I promise to be good. If I can," he added, in a private whisper, as he trotted along next to Dul Dul.

"Oh, how I wish Pitki was with us!" sighed Dul Dul, thinking of his friend again.

5

A Joyful Meeting

You may remember that we left Pitki fast asleep in Mama Bird's nest, while little Cheep Cheep kept a watch over him.

Mrs Squirrel came up to the nest, and Cheep Cheep began chirruping in such an excited way that

Pitki woke up. He sat up and gazed round him. His eyes fell on Mrs Squirrel. He rubbed them in surprise and looked again. No, it wasn't a dream; it really was his mother!

"Mama!" he squeaked, and flung himself into her paws.

"Pitki, you little rascal!" cried his mother, hugging him warmly, but trying to sound a bit stern, "you don't know how unhappy you made me!"

"Oh Mama! I am sorry. I promise I won't run away again. But oh! I must, I really must find Dul Dul first."

"Who is Dul Dul?" asked Cheep Cheep.

"He's my friend. He helped me and fed me and gave me a ride and saved me from the bullfrog and ..."

"But who is he?" chorused the other three. "Why, don't you know? He's a magic clay horse. And Mama, he must be so sad, because after he had rescued me from the lily pool, a horrid hawk carried me off."

"Oh! Pitki, my poor little pet!" cried Mrs Squirrel, quite forgetting to be cross with him. "But now, come along, we must go home. Thank you so much, Mama Bird."

"Mama, I'm feeling very hungry," said Pitki.

"So am I, Mama," chirruped Cheep Cheep. Mama Bird flew off to bring another grub for her chick, while Pitki went with his mother to a grand feast of nuts.

"Pitki," called Cheep Cheep as he was going, "please let me meet Dul Dul when you find him. Promise?"

"I promise," said Pitki, "we shall go to find him together."

6

Pilla In A Fix

Pilla trotted quietly by Dul Dul for about ten yards. Then he saw the lily pool, and could not manage to keep still any more.

"There it is! Look! Ooh ... I'm thirsty," he barked, and before Garbar knew what was happening, Pilla turned three somersaults in the air, two backwards, one forwards, and in a jiffy, was streaking along to the edge of the pool.

Dul Dul couldn't help laughing at him. He looked like a big speckled ball rolling down the hill and Garbar shook his head.

"I'm sure he'll fall right into it," he said gloomily.

"I hope not," said Dul Dul, "old Mr Bullfrog will not be easy to get rid of a second time, I'm certain."

Pilla chased along happily, when suddenly his foot caught in a root. Over and over and over he went, gathering slush and moss and pebbles all over him as he rolled.

Halfway down the slope was a thick, prickly bush, and right into the middle of it rolled the messy little ball that was Pilla! There he was stuck fast in the thorns.

"Help! Help!" squeaked the wriggly ball. Dul Dul and Garbar raced down as fast as they could to pull him out. But the bush was too thick.

"Stay still, Pilla, or the prickles will hurt you more," said Dul Dul.

Old Garbar laughed, "Now, this will teach you a lesson! You stay here. I shall go down, have a drink and then I'll come back, munch up this bush and get you out. Till then, cheerio!" And he ambled off.

Garbar took a long time to go down to the lily pool. There he had a cool drink and washed his face and straggly beard. Then he slowly ambled up the slope to the prickly bush where Pilla was stuck fast among the thorns.

"Ha! Now I'm hungry," said Garbar, "so don't worry, Pilla, we shall have you out in a minute."

Sure enough, to Dul Dul's great surprise, Garbar munched and munched at the big, thorny bush. He ate the leaves and twigs and thorns and prickles! He ate and ate till there was nothing left of the bush but a few, bare stumps! And among the stumps was Pilla!

Dul Dul and Garbar managed to pull out the pup. He was still full of mud and covered with burrs and pebbles. While Dul Dul began pulling off the burrs, Garbar nosed around the bush for another mouthful. Something jabbed him!

"Ouch!" he cried. "Pilla, have you left your tail behind in the prickles?"

"Oh, my poor tail" yapped Pilla. "Let me see." He also peered into the stumps. There, sure enough, lay a small, prickly, curled-up ball.

"You sillies," said Dul Dul laughing, "that's not Pilla's tail." And he held the pup's tail up for them to see. It was firmly stuck to Pilla's body.

"Oh, goody good! That's not my tail!" barked Pilla. "But what is it?"

All three of them watched the prickly ball closely. Slowly it moved. A little snout came out from one end. Two beady eyes appeared. Suddenly it moved off into a hole in the ground.

"Why! It's Prickles the Hedgehog!" cried Pilla. "I must have sat on him when I was in the bush. I feel quite sore!"

Just then they heard a little voice above them calling, "Dul Dul!"

7

The Lucky Dip Surprise

"Dul Dul," chirped a little voice. "Dool-doo-oo-oo-"
and it seemed to fade away.

Pilla, Garbar and Dul Dul looked round, looked
up, under the bush, into a tree.

Suddenly, something fell on Pilla's back with a soft
plop! He gave a leap that landed him straight into
Garbar's horns; Garbar shook his head and tossed
him right under Dul Dul's nose! For a while it looked
as though an exciting game of dodge-ball was being
played! Dul Dul, however, put a stop to all that by
firmly though gently, placing a hoof on Pilla's head.

Garbar and Dul Dul then peered at the limp little
object that seemed to be glued onto Pilla's back.

"Why! It's a tiny little chick-a-dee," grunted
Garbar. "Where on earth did she come from?"

"How did she know my name?" added Dul Dul,
trying to pick her out of Pilla's tangled coat.

"Oo ... Hee ... hee ... you're tickling me, hee, hee!"
giggled Pilla, wriggling about and making it very
difficult for Dul Dul to get the birdie's little claws out
of Pilla's messy curls, which were still sticky with
slush and burrs.

"Be still, you scallywag, or I'll pin you down with
my horns, I will!" threatened Garbar.

"Cheep, cheep, cheep," said the bird faintly, as Dul Dul put her safely on the grass.

"What's your name?" asked Dul Dul.

"Cheep Cheep, Cheep Cheep ..."

"Don't cry. You're safe. Just tell us your name?"

"Cheep Cheep," chirped the chick again.

"That's her name, silly," yapped Pilla, glad to be able to prove how clever he was, for a change. "She is Cheep Cheep."

"Oh, I see," said Dul Dul. "How did you get here and who told you my name?"

"Pitki sent me. He's waiting in a tree near the lily pool."

Cheep Cheep was so tired after her very first solo flight that she could not flap another wing!

"Never mind, Cheep Cheep," said Dul Dul, "you may ride on my back. Just tell us where we can find Pitki."

All of them set off down the hill towards the lily pool. Pilla was kept right at the back by Garbar.

When they got to the pool Pilla ran off to have a drink of water, while Dul Dul and Garbar were directed to a large tree by Cheep Cheep.

"Pitki has been very ill, so his mummy would not let him get off the tree," she explained. "That is why I had to fly to you all by myself."

"You are a very brave birdie," muttered Garbar, kindly.

"Oh! I was frightened. I got so tired. But I love this pony ride, Dul Dul!" she added.

As they reached the big tree, Pitki, who had been waiting and wondering what had happened, saw them. He got so excited, he forgot all about being ill or weak and gave a leap right on to Dul Dul, knocking poor Cheep Cheep off his back! What a happy, noisy meeting it was! They all had to get to know one another. Pilla came bouncing up and he, too, met Pitki.

"Oh Dul Dul," cried Pitki, "let's never lose each other again!"

"Let's all stay together," yapped Pilla.

"Me too, me too!" chirped Cheep Cheep. "Now, now," said Garbar gruffly, "less noise; more sense! Where can we live?"

"Why shouldn't we build a little hut under this tree?" suggested Dul Dul. "Cheep Cheep and Pitki will live above us and the three of us, who can't climb trees, can stay just beneath them."

"Oh grand!" shouted Pilla.

"Good grief! Shall I have to put up with this rubber ball every day?" teased Garbar.

But he did not really mean it and soon all the friends were busy gathering branches and bricks, palm leaves and mud to build a lovely little chummery beneath the banyan tree.

8

Setting Up House

At last the little house was ready! It had walls of bamboo, a roof thatched with big leaves, a floor of mud and coloured pebbles, while the door was a large piece of bark, carefully removed from a fallen log by Pitki and Garbar.

Inside, the three animals had made themselves very comfortable. In one corner was Garbar's straw

bed and a place to store grass and leaves; Dul Dul preferred a hard mattress, so he had placed a flat stone in another corner and just covered it with a palm leaf; Pilla who did not dare place his cot near Garbar's, had found a torn, old, warm coat in a hedge by the park and had carried it back, full of glee, rolled it up into an untidy bundle, put it next to Dul Dul's bed and curled himself up in the middle of it!

He looked so happy and good that even Garbar had to smile at him!

Just behind his cot, Pilla had dug a little hole, in which he planned to hide any bones he found. He did this while Garbar was away. In fact, he even kept it a secret from Dul Dul! Just as he had dug it nice and round and smooth and had patted down the mud neatly, Cheep Cheep flew in with a branch of wild, red berries in her beak.

She dropped the berries in surprise. "What are you up to, Pilla?" she cheeped.

"Oh brother!" yapped the pup. "Now you'll tell everyone. Girls! They are pests!"

"I'm not, I'm not," chirruped Cheep Cheep, in tears. "I-w-won't tell anyone. But-what-?"

"It's just a place to keep my bones in, silly. Stop crying! Where are the others?" asked Pilla.

"They're just coming. Oh Pilla, just think! We are going to have a party. Dul Dul said so. Everyone is bringing something," Cheep Cheep replied.

"Then I must be off to fetch something too," said Pilla bouncing out.

Pilla ran, helter-skelter, as fast as his legs would carry him, out of the park, through the little white gate, back onto the crowded bazaar street where he had first met Dul Dul. He felt sure that the nicest things he could bring to the party were to be found in the gutter behind the butcher's shop, the window of the bakery and beside the kitchen of the *halwai*!

He found a nice, juicy bone in the drain and managed to snatch a fine, fat loaf from the baker's window. Feeling quite pleased with himself he ran round to the *halwai*'s shop. Just as he squeezed himself

past some bulls, which were nosing round a basket of greens and then over the feet of a fat woman, who sat on the ground selling onions, Pilla suddenly found himself caught between the spindly legs of an old man. He tried to wriggle out, the old man gave a sort of gasp and both of them rolled over onto the road.

Pilla got up, shook himself, then looked round for his loaf and bone. He turned and saw that the old man was gazing at a heap of broken clay pots, shaking his head and weeping.

Being a kind-hearted pup, Pilla bounced up to the man, licked his straggly beard and asked, "Why are you so sad? Cheer up! I'll give you half my loaf. "

The old man patted the little dog's head but shook his own, "It's no good. Ever since my magic clay horse ran away, my luck has gone, too!"

"My goodness! Do you know Dul Dul?" yapped Pilla. "If so, your luck is in. Come on, come on, Baba*ji*! I'll take you to him. What a lovely surprise for the party!"

An Unexpected Guest

Dul Dul, Garbar, Pitki and Cheep Cheep were waiting for Pilla to begin the party.

"Dear, dear! That young pup will never improve," said Garbar, soberly.

"There he is!" twittered Cheep Cheep, excitedly. "He is not alone."

"Oh my! That's Sonoo the Potter. He must be coming to drag me back to the bazaar!" cried Dul Dul, in panic. "He'll sell me, he will! What shall I do?"

"Hide!" whispered Pitki.

Dul Dul hid under a pile of hay that Garbar had stacked in a corner.

Pilla and Sonoo came up, watched by the other friends.

"Dul Dul, where are you? I've brought a surprise for your party — oh!" Pilla's voice broke off sharply, as Garbar butted first him and then Sonoo. Pitki and Cheep Cheep also attacked them.

Poor old Sonoo sat on the floor, trying to save his head from Cheep Cheep's sharp pecks.

"Oh! Oh!" he wept. "I came to meet my dear little magic clay horse, for I thought he would bring me luck, but all I get are blows."

Dul Dul felt very sorry for Sonoo, when he heard him weep. He jumped out of the hay.

"Please don't cry, Baba*ji*. Here I am," he said.

Sonoo threw his arms around the horse's neck and wept for joy. All the others were happy and excited too!

"Please don't sell me in the bazaar," Dul Dul said. "Stay, here with us and we will look after you."

"Yes! Yes! Please stay with us," chorused the others.

This made Sonoo very happy. Sonoo had no family; he was growing old; no one bought the clay pots he made, so he was a lonely old man. Only one thing bothered him.

"How will I earn my living here?" he asked "Where will I make my pots?"

Pitki suddenly remembered something. "Dul Dul!" he cried, "there is a lot of lovely, sticky clay at the bottom of the lily pool. I felt it when I fell in! Remember?"

"Yes, I do. You were coated with clay when Mr Bullfrog fished you out," said Dul Dul.

"That's fine!" grunted Garbar. "Let's go and get some clay. Don't you worry, Babaji. You can make your pots right here!"

"We will make you a hut just next to our own," added Pilla, very excited, since it was he who had found old Sonoo.

"How good you are," quavered the Potter, quite overcome by all their kindness. "I know! I shall make beautiful clay toys that look exactly like each one of you, my dear young friends!"

And so it came to pass that Sonoo the Potter, who lived in the forest hut with his magic clay horse and his forest friends, grew to be very famous for his wonderful toys. All the village children wanted a small horse or a grumpy mud goat; a perky clay squirrel or a funny little dog; a sweet painted bird or a lop-eared rabbit, made by Sonoo.

Every Monday was market day. Sonoo would collect the toys he had made and put them into a basket, which he would then put onto Garbar's back. With Pilla trotting at his heels, Sonoo would walk beside Garbar to the bazaar. Dul Dul and the others would wait for them to return. What rejoicing there would be when the basket came back empty!

Sonoo would often buy presents for each of his little friends: a juicy bone for Pilla, carrots for old Garbar, nuts for Mrs Squirrel and Pitki, fruit for Mama Bird and Cheep Cheep and beautiful, red ornamental harnesses, with small bells attached to it, for Dul Dul!

All the animals would hover round Sonoo while he moulded the clay on his whirling wheel, wondering whether his clever fingers would turn out an odd sort of Garbar or a funny kind of Pilla! They all would help him paint his toys in bright colours. But try as he would, never again was old Sonoo able to make another toy that came alive! Dul Dul remained, to the end, the only magic clay horse!

The Adventures
of Pilla the Pup

To the memory of
The Vanished Pu's—Nano, Zaza, Bendy

1

Pilla Looks For Fun

It was a lovely, sunny morning. Little Cheep Cheep, the birdling, was chirping a gay spring song waiting for her friend, Pitki the Squirrel, to come and join her. She wanted to play hide-and-seek in the Big Banyan tree.

But Pitki was very hungry and he was busy nibbling nuts in the cosy little hollow at the bottom of the tree trunk.

"Cheep cheep-chee-chirr-rrrr," sang Cheep Cheep, her song getting higher and shriller with every chirrup.

"Oh, shurrup!" growled a nasty, cross voice. "Must you make such a horrid noise?" asked Pilla as came out of his hut. He sat under the branch beneath Cheep Cheep and looked at her with such a scowl that the little bird got quite frightened.

"Oh Pilla, whatever is the matter with you?" he asked. "Are you ill? Will you play tag with me?"

"I don't play with silly girls," was the cross reply, "and do be quiet. My head is feeling all muggy with your cheep cheep-cheeping."

"My, you are as grumpy as Garbar the Goat," replied Cheep Cheep pertly, "only lie is old and his bones pain, so he has a reason for being cross. Whatever is the matter with you, Pilla?"

But Pilla lay down with his head on his paws and his curly tail flat and straight behind him, and would not answer.

Just then Pitki came out frisking his tail. "Come on, Cheep Cheep," he squeaked, "let's be off!" And not looking where he was jumping, he gave a leap and landed bang on Pilla's nose.

"Look out, stupid," yapped Pilla. "You mousy chump!" he added.

"'Pilla, I am sorry," said Pitki, very upset at being called mousy, which is the worst thing you can ever call a squirrel. "I thought you had gone with Garbar and Sonoo the Potter to the Monday market in town."

"They would not take me," sighed Pilla.

"Is that why you are feeling cross?" asked Cheep Cheep.

"Oh, I don't care for the silly market," replied Pilla grandly.

But Cheep Cheep nodded wisely at Pitki and quietly the two little friends made off to another part of the park to play.

Pilla gave a sigh. He had nothing to do. And being a pup full of bounce, this was the hardest punishment for him. Of course, he knew it was his own fault.

"Oh bother!" Pilla growled. "I am so bored. But I don't care. I'm off to look for some fun, all on my own."

He jumped up, gave a bounce or two, curled up his tail and putting his nose in the air, trotted off down the path that led to the town.

2

Meeting Old Friends

That morning Sonoo had been getting ready to take his mud toys to market to sell when he found his basket missing. He looked all round his small hut, but it was not there. He then went over to the little hut next to his. Here lived his dear friends. There was Dul Dul the Magic Clay Horse, Garbar and Pilla.

Long ago, Dul Dul had plopped off Sonoo's wheel and run off into the wide, wide world. He had found himself in a big, pretty park and here he had made some very good friends. They were Pilla, a black and white patched, woolly ball of bounce and trouble, and the old goat whose name Garbar will tell you all about what he was like. But under his cross manner and grumbly words, Garbar hid a very kind heart. Dul Dul found him to be a wonderful pal.

Dul Dul had also rescued Pitki when that naughty chap had run away from home. And Pitki, of course, had brought Cheep Cheep to join the happy band.

But it was Pilla who had come across old Sonoo while he was on one of his jaunts in the bazaar. Sonoo had been old and sad and all alone. So Pilla, who was a kind pup and very friendly most of the time, had taken Sonoo back with him to live in the park.

All had gone well. The friends had made a fine hut for Sonoo next to their own. Sonoo used to make mud toys from the sticky clay found at the bottom of the lily pool in the middle of the park, and every Monday he packed the toys into his basket. Garbar carried the basket on his back, Sonoo walked beside him, while Pilla trotted at his heels. But now, here was Monday, and no basket could be found.

"Garbar, have you seen my basket?" asked Sonoo.

"Basket? No. Ask Dul Dul," said Garbar, in his usual "shorthand" manner.

"Basket?" echoed Dul Dul. "Why isn't it in your hut, Babaji? I am certain I saw it there last evening."

But Pilla, curled up in his corner, just buried his head in his tail looking like a big, shaggy powder puff.

Sonoo looked at Pilla.

Garbar glared at Pilla.

Dul Dul stared and stared at Pilla. Pilla tried to wriggle right under his warm rag, but never said a word.

"Ahem," said Sonoo,

"Grr-uph," coughed Garbar.

"Aha!" cried Dul Dul.

"No, no, no," yapped Pilla, "I didn't do it. I mean, I did not mean ... I mean I did not think ..." and up he bounced, shaking his head and wagging his tail.

"You never think," Garbar scolded. "Stand still, silly!"

"Now Pilla," said Dul Dul quietly, "do be still and answer properly."

"Oh Dul Dul," cried the Pup, "I dug for a bone, and I looked for a bone, and I hunted, and nosed, and scratched and scouted, and ..."

"Well, well, doesn't matter," sighed Sonoo. "We know all. You found the basket instead."

"Oh Baba*ji*," yelped Pilla, "my tummy was all rumbly and my jaws all chewy and my teeth all rattly and ..."

"You are too chattery," finished Garbar.

Pilla flopped down.

"I think Baba*ji*," said Dul Dul, "we must leave Pilla to think, and Garbar and I can help you to carry the toys to town."

"That may be best," replied Sonoo. "We can buy a basket in the bazaar."

And that is why Pilla was so cross and sad all morning before he made up his mind to go off all on his own to look for some fun.

3

Pilla Finds Trouble

Pilla went briskly along the narrow lane that led to the bazaar. He was sure old Sonoo would not send him back once he had joined his friends. Feeling quite happy and gay he gave a hop and a bounce and turned a quick somersault just for fun.

As he got to the butcher's shop at the corner, he stopped. There on the window sill lay a big bone. Pilla gave a quick look round. No one was in sight. Then he shook his head. He must be good. But he could not help staring at the bone.

"I shall only take a teeny sniff," he thought, "Just one weeny, snuffly sniff," and he put his front paws up on the window sill.

"Chee-ow! Hee-ow! Mee-ow!" snarled a nasty voice. "Catchee thief!"

"Piaoo! Miaoo! Chiaoo!" screeched a second voice. "Patchee thief!"

Two shadowy forms fell from the roof straight onto Pilla's paws.

"Ouch!" yelled the pup. "Let me go."

"Nee-ow! See-ow! Mee-ow!"

"Diaoo! Siaoo! Niaoo!"

"Woof! Woof! Woof!" barked Pilla struggling madly, as the two nasty creatures clawed at his ears. "One at a time. Fight fair!"

For a while nothing could be seen, but a mass of fur and a mess of claws and paws and snapping jaws and nothing could be heard, but hissing and spitting and yelping.

"Out! Out! Off with you. Horrid things! Off with you," shrilled a new voice, as the butcher's wife came running out with a large broom in her hands.

"Out! Off! Away!" and she swept the fighting animals right into an open drain.

"Mee-ow!" screeched one, leaping from the drain onto a lamp post.

"Chiaoo!" snarled another, creeping under a dustbin.

"Wouch!" barked Pilla and he gave a jump which landed him, plop, onto the back of a dhobi's donkey. The donkey was laden with two big bundles of freshly washed clothes. When Pilla landed on him he got such a fright and he bolted down the bazaar.

"Oh! Oh! My clothes. Come back! Get off! Stop! Go away," cried the poor fat dhobi, getting all mixed up.

Pilla clung on to the knot between the bundles and snuggled down, wiping his wet coat on the fresh white sheets. The donkey clattered on, bumping into cyclists and knocking down the smart policeman in the centre; he was curling his moustache with one hand and swinging his cane with the other.

"Hey! Stop! Wretch!" cried the policeman, getting up and whirling his cane wildly.

"Stop!" cried the dhobi, wobbling along behind.

"Gee-up," cried Pilla, enjoying the fun, "Giddy-up! Hi-up and off we go!"

4

The Donkey Has A Feast

"After them!" yelled the policeman.

"Stop them!" cried the dhobi.

The race was on! All the little boys joined the chase. The bazaar dogs stopped sniffing round the stalls; the vegetable sellers left their baskets; even the old bull got up and ambled along behind.

"Woof, woof!" barked Pilla. "Giddy-up, old long-ears. Turn off to the right," he added, pulling the

donkey's right ear. The dhobi's donkey was puffing and panting like an old train going up a hill. He puffed and panted and huffed and hawed as he turned first right, then left, then right again, as Pilla directed by pulling his ears.

At last they turned into a gate that opened into a big bungalow's garden. Here the donkey came on a patch of bright yellow flowers. He put his front legs out together and stopped dead. Pilla flew off over his head. The donkey without wasting a second began munching the flowers greedily.

"Good brakes," cried Pilla, laughing as he picked himself up. "That was a joyride friend. Thank you for saving me." Then he gave a funny little bounce and a bow to the donkey. But the donkey never said a word. He just went munch, munch, crunch, crunch at the flowers.

Pilla sat down with a bump. He stared at the donkey. Never had he seen anyone eat so much, so fast. When the last yellow flower had disappeared the donkey looked up and saw a patch of blue cornflowers just beyond. Off he went and soon the blue flowers began to go the way of the yellow ones.

"Nathu! Mangu! Jangu!" cried a voice, as a door banged in the distance. "Nathu, watch out. There is a donkey in the flower beds. Oh my, oh dear! Mangu, Jangu. Catch the wretch!" and, pitter patter, out came a lady on very high heels with an umbrella in her hands. "Nathu!"

"Here Memsahib," called a voice. "I'll get him. It's our dhobi's donkey. He has brought our wash."

"Where is the dhobi?"

"Not here, Memsahib. Hey, you rascal," cried Nathu, running out and clutching at the bundles on the donkey's back.

"Gee-up friend. Time we were off," cried Pilla, running towards the gate. The donkey gave a heave, Nathu gave a tug. The bundles fell off and the donkey galloped after Pilla, not stopping to look behind.

5

The Sad Story Of Ladhu The Donkey

Pilla shot out of the gate and made straight for the park. He felt he had had enough fun to last him quite a while. He could hear the donkey running behind him.

When he came to the edge of the park, Pilla took a deep breath and slowed down to a walk. The donkey came up to him. They both made for a shady tree and sat down together.

But Pilla soon bounced up.

"You must let me thank you again," he began, "now that you are not too busy. Thank you, friend, and tell me your name."

At this the donkey shook his long ears and burst into tears. He bawled at the top of his voice. "Hoaar, whoar! Hoar, woaar!" he wept as the tears poured down his long, sad face.

"Oh dear. I am sorry. Do stop. Don't cry. Oh dear, what have I done to upset you?" cried poor Pilla, feeling very bad though he could not make out what he had done wrong this time. The donkey took no notice of Pilla but howled even louder. Pilla could not help thinking that whatever his new friend did, he did with all his might. First he ran, and then he ate and now he cried. So he made up his mind to just sit and wait till the donkey came to the end of his tears.

"Hoarr! Whoarr! Whrrap!" and as suddenly as he had begun his horrid noise, the donkey stopped. He hung his ears down and kept absolutely quiet.

"Ahem," said Pilla softly. "Aha! Er ... may I ... er ... are you ... I mean will you tell me your name? That is ... I mean you know ... not if it upsets you ... er. I mean if you ..." and Pilla got all mixed up as usual, trying to be extra polite.

"Haw! Haw! Haw!" laughed the donkey gaping at the pup. "Hee, hee, hee, hee! Haw! Haw! Haw-aw-aw," and he shouted and guffawed and rolled about in the oddest fit of giggles that Pilla had ever heard or seen.

"Oh bother," thought Pilla. "Now I'll have to be still again till he finishes this one too." So he sat down

and watched the donkey as he gulped and giggled and "heed and hawed" to his heart's content.

Suddenly the haw, haw, hee, hee, stopped. The donkey sat still and silent.

Pilla was very glad. But he was in a fix. He did not know how to begin. He did not want to start another long song-and-dance by his new friend.

"Ladhu! Oh Ladhu! Oh rascal! Where are you Ladhu?" Pilla bounced up as he saw the fat dhobi running up to them with a big stick in his hands.

"Aha! There you are rascal! You devil," cried the dhobi, and he began to beat the poor donkey with the stick and tug at his ears with his other hand.

"Yap! Yap!" barked Pilla. "Stop it, you nasty, fat bully," and he snapped at the dhobi's ankles. The donkey just sat on his haunches and refused to budge.

"Thank goodness he is sticking again to one point," thought Pilla, biting and barking and rushing round the dhobi.

"Get away, you dirty dog," cried the dhobi.

This nasty name made Pilla so angry that he caught the dhobi's dhoti in his teeth and gave a strong tug.

"Ooo-eee!" cried the dhobi, dropping his stick and clutching at his dhoti with both hands. "Let go, wretch," and he began running away as fast as his fat legs would carry him out of the park. Pilla followed, yapping at his heels, till the dhobi had gone far away. Then Pilla turned back to his friend.

The donkey sat quite silent and still. Pilla came up to him and giving him a friendly lick on one ear said, "Now I know your name, pal. You are Ladhu, the donkey. And I also know your sad story. Never mind Ladhu, you can stay with me. I will be your friend. We can both help each other. What do you say to that?"

Ladhu never said a word instead he gave a yawn and a sigh and before Pilla could wag a tail, Ladhu lay down and fell fast asleep.

"Well that's that," thought Pilla, shaking his head at his odd friend. "I better have rest too."

6

The Bully In The Big Banyan

While Pilla was looking for fun in the town, Cheep Cheep and Pitki were also having a good time playing the game they liked best. This was hide-and-seek in the Big Banyan. The Big Banyan stood just next to the tree in which the friends lived. Mama Bird had a nest high above, where Cheep Cheep stayed with her, while Pitki and his mother lived in a hollow in the middle of the trunk. Dul Dul's hut and Sonoo's too, were built just under this tree. It was a very pretty tree. But it was not as much fun as the Big Banyan. The Big Banyan was the oldest tree in the park. It had many many hanging roots that swung down from its branches and many of these roots had reached the ground and become trees on their own. So the Big Banyan was almost like a small forest. At the bottom of the central trunk, was the hollow in which Pitki hid his nuts.

Now if you have read about Dul Dul and his pals in "Dul Dul The Magic Clay Horse", you will remember that Dul Dul found Pitki in this very hollow. And you will also know that the Big Banyan was the home of Kaa the Crow, and Kaa was a very mean bird. Pitki and Cheep Cheep knew that it was not a safe place to play in. But this did not stop them. They felt very brave, hiding-and-seeking right under the beak of Kaa, the crow.

It was Pitki's turn to hide. He scampered along a branch till he came to the very tip of it. Here a bunch of leaves made a fine hiding nook. He crept inside the leaves and squeaked out, "Coo-ee! Find me, Cheep Cheep."

Cheep Cheep flew from one branch to another but could not find Pitki.

"Coo-ee," chuckled Pitki. "Coo-ee! Coo-ee!"

Now, just above the branch where the squirrel was hiding, Ma Kaa was sitting on her nest hatching her eggs. She was very tired. Kaa had gone off to find some food and she was waiting for him to return to take his turn at egg-sitting while she had a chance to stretch her wings. Pitki's shrill, "Coo-ee! Coo-ee!" made her cross. She looked over the edge of her nest and saw a bit of grey fluff in the leaves below. It was Pitki's tail.

"Coo-ee!" called Pitki again.

Ma Kaa got off her eggs and made a dive at the squirrel's tail.

"Ouch!" cried Pitki. "What are you doing, Cheep Cheep?"

"Kaa! Kaa! Kaa!" cawed Ma Kaa, in a hoarse voice.

In a second, dozens of crows all cawing, "Kaa! Kaa! Kaa!" came flocking to the branch where Pitki was hiding. The poor little chap was terribly frightened. He tried to creep under the branch but Ma Kaa had caught his tail in her beak and would not let go. Pitki dug his claws into the bark and clung on with all his might, while the din of the cawing made him quite dizzy.

"Kaa! Kaa! Kaa!" cried the crows.

Cheep Cheep heard the battle cry of the crows. At once she guessed what had happened.

"Oh dear! Whatever shall I do?" she whimpered. "No one is home to help us. I better fly off to find Dul Dul," and away she flew across the park.

7

Pilla And Ladhu Join Forces

As Cheep Cheep flew towards the town, she kept her eyes on the park below. But she could not see Sonoo or Garbar or Dul Dul returning from the market. Just then she saw the oddest sight. Under a tree near the edge of the park, lay a donkey, fast asleep and snoring so loudly that Cheep Cheep could hear the rumbling up in the air. Next to the donkey, with his head on the snorer's tummy, lay Pilla. The pup kept bobbing up and down like a cork on the waves of a rising and falling sea tide.

"Goodness! Whatever is Pilla up to now?" thought Cheep Cheep as she flew towards the odd couple. She landed on the donkey's back. The donkey kept snoring and Pilla kept bobbing. Cheep Cheep hopped up to Pilla and gave him a peck.

"Wake up, Pilla," she cheeped. "Pilla, do get up. Pitki is in a trap. The crows have got him."

Pilla bounced up in a trice. "My, I thought I was dreaming. Cheep Cheep, wait. We must take Ladhu with us."

"Who is Ladhu?" asked the birdie.

"My new friend. But I must be careful. I never know what he will do next. And if we are to save

Pitki, it must be the right thing. I can't think of what I should do. My brain is all sleepy."

Pilla thought it might be a good idea to shake up his brain a bit to get him thinking again. So he began bouncing up and down chanting, "Ladhu wake up. We must save Pitki. Ladhu wake up. We must save Pitki."

An extra big bounce, landed him on Ladhu's back with a bump. In a jiffy Ladhu stopped snoring, jumped up, and before Cheep Cheep could chirp a hello, was off at a gallop with Pilla clinging onto his back.

"Giddy-up!" cried Pilla. "Here we come, Pitki, Down with Kaa and all the crows!"

Cheep Cheep flew above the charging steed. Pilla turned Ladhu by a lug of the ears and off they went.

When they were almost there, Cheep Cheep saw Sonoo, Garbar and Dul Dul, returning from the town.

"Dul Dul, Garbar, Dul Dul. Baba*ji*!" she cheeped loudly.

"Goodness," said old Sonoo. "I hear Cheep Cheep's voice."

"There she is," shouted Dul Dul, "but what on earth is that funny animal running so crazily beneath her?"

"Ha! Had to be Pilla on an ass. The silly ass!" mumbled Garbar.

"Dul Dul! Baba*ji*! Come quick, Pitki. Come. Kaa. Come," cheeped Cheep Cheep as she flew on towards the Big Banyan.

"'Let's hurry, friends," said Dul Dul, and the three of them began to follow Cheep Cheep as fast as they could go.

8

The Merry-Go-Round

All Pilla could think of while he was being carried along like a knight on a charger was how he could get Ladhu to stop at the right place. He could hear the "Kaa! Kaa! Kaa!" of the crows getting louder and louder as they got close to the Big Banyan tree.

"Poor little Pitki," thought Pilla. "She must be having a bad time. I must think of a way to stop Ladhu."

They had just got to the Big Banyan and could see the crows circling round one branch cawing, "Kaa! Kaa! Kaa!" as they dived at the bunch of leaves at the end.

"Well, here goes," said Pilla. He crept up Ladhu's neck and just as they passed under the branch where Pitki was being attacked, Pilla stretched out his front legs and clapped his paws on top of Ladhu's eyes. It worked like magic. Ladhu put both front feet out together and stopped dead. The jerk threw Pilla over his head.

"This is becoming quite a circus act with me," thought Pilla, as he picked himself up. He turned to look at his friend. Ladhu had put his head down and was busy munching the thick green grass.

"Good enough," Pilla smiled.

Sonoo, Garbar and Dul Dul came up just then. The cries of the crows were quite deafening.

"Kaa! Kaa! Kaa!"

"Pitki, are you alright? Pitki, we are all coming to help you, Pitki," cried all the friends in chorus; all except Ladhu who was still busy munching.

"Dul Dul," cried a small squeaky voice from above.

"Good! Pitki hang on. Just a minute now," called Dul Dul.

"But Dul Dul, what can we do?" whispered Pilla. "How can we reach Pitki? None of us can climb. Baba*ji*, can you climb the tree?"

Poor Sonoo looked up sadly. "It's too high for me," he said,

"Goats can climb," suggested Dul Dul.

"Not trees," replied Garbar shortly.

"Wait," cried Dul Dul. "Can goats climb on top of a donkey?"

Garbar looked at the munching donkey that had not even looked up at any of the friends. "Greedy ass," he thought to himself. Then to Dul Dul he said, "Yes," and with that he promptly jumped on top of Ladhu's back before Pilla could warn anyone about his friend's odd habits. No sooner had Garbar got on to Ladhu's back than the donkey flew off at a gallop. Garbar jerked forward and almost fell. To save himself he caught Ladhu's right ear in his mouth and clung to it. Ladhu turned right, around the banyan tree and since Garbar would not let go, the donkey kept turning right and began running round and round the banyan, in a dizzy circle.

"What now?" thought Pilla in despair. "How on earth shall I stop this new act?"

But he need not have bothered. As soon as the crows heard the din below and saw a strange creature dashing madly round their tree, in and out of the hanging roots, they all stopped diving at the hidden squirrel and swooped down on the whirling object. "Kaa! Kaa! Kaa!" they cried.

No sooner had they come low enough to join the merry-go-round, than all the friends joined in the chase. Sonoo ran after them whirling his empty baskets. Pilla bounced and snapped at them. Dul Dul snorted and charged at them.

Garbar did not enjoy his ride. As the crows flew in front of Ladhu, the donkey slowed down his headlong rush. This gave Garbar his chance. He jumped off and began butting the crows. What a jumble there was!

In the meantime, seeing the crows were all busy, Cheep Cheep flew up to the branch where Pitki was hiding. "Come along, Pitki, you can run away now. But come quickly."

Pale and still trembling with fear, Pitki scrambled out of his hiding place and scampered down the nearest hanging root as fast as he could. Ma Kaa had pulled off all the fur at the end of his tail and the tip was quite bare and sore. As soon as he was on the ground, Pitki made off for home, not waiting to see how the chase would end.

The crows were tired of being beaten and butted, so they all flew off. Ma Kaa returned to her nest. Ladhu, who could hardly see where he was going, bumped into a swinging root. He stopped running and stood quite still.

Sonoo, Garbar, Dul Dul and Pilla all came up to the donkey. Pilla bounced up and gave his pal another lick. "Good work, Ladhu. You saved Pitki from the crows. And we saved you," he added. "Now we can all be friends."

"Hice-oop!" panted the donkey, trying to get his breath back. "Hicc ... hicc ... hicc-oop!"

"Oh, dear," said Pilla. "Now he is sure to have a long, long spell of hiccups. Well. In the meantime, I better tell you all about him."

And so, while the rest sat down near the hiccupping donkey, Pilla told them his tale.

9

The Butterfly Waltz

"Pilla," said Dul Dul, one sunny morning about a week later, "I have to go down to the lily pool to fetch some more clay for Baba*ji*. Would you like to come with me?"

"I'd love to come," and so saying, Pilla bounced up from his corner. "But isn't Baba*ji* coming too?"

"He was not too well last night," said Dul Dul, "so I thought we should do it for him."

"Old bones. Like mine," said Garbar gruffly, from his straw bed.

"But how can we dig the clay out of the pool?" asked Pilla.

"We can take Babaj's rake with us. If you help I think I can manage to rake up some and we can fill up a bucket or two with it."

"Do you think we could take Ladhu with us, Dul Dul?" asked Pilla. "Do let us take him. Please let us."

"That ass?" scoffed Garbar.

"He's not an ass," began Pilla, "Well I mean ... I know he is ... but he is not an ass ... that is ... he is not stupid ..." and Pilla got all mixed up as usual, trying to speak up for his friend.

"Hrmph," snorted Garbar. "Sleeps out. Must be stupid. Is an ass."

"Now, never mind," put in Dul Dul quickly. "He can come and help carry the buckets."

"Oh goodee-good " shouted Pilla, jumping up and dashing out to tell Ladhu the good news.

"Hope he won't fall in!" said Garbar.

"Who? Where?" asked Dul Dul.

"Ass. Lily pool," replied Garbar shortly.

Dul Dul laughed, "It will certainly give that bad-tempered bullfrog a fright if Ladhu does take a dip in his pool. He is always croaking rude remarks at us when we go there. Did I ever tell you how Pitki fell into the pond and the bullfrog ...?"

"Yes." Garbar cut Dul Dul short. "Heard it. Twice."

"Oh," said Dul Dul rather crestfallen. Because he liked telling this story very much.

Just then Pilla bounced back into the hut.

"Come on, Dul Dul," he called.

"Is Ladhu ready?" asked Dul Dul.

"Well, ye-es. That is he is almost ready ... I mean he will be ready ... at least ..."

"What is he doing now?" asked Garbar.

"Well ... he is ... that is, I think he is ... oh dear, to tell you the truth, Dul Dul, I don't know what he is doing."

"Why? Has he gone away?" asked Dul Dul.

"Oh no," replied Pilla, "He is very much here. And I think that it looks as if ... I mean he is trying ... I think he is dancing!" shouted Pilla in despair.

"Dancing? That ass?" said Garbar getting up.

"This we must see," chortled Dul Dul "Where is he, Pilla?"

"Just behind our hut," said Pilla. "Come along! Come and see him. He looks so funny!"

Cheep Cheep flew in, "Oh, Dul Dul, do come and join us. We are having such fun. Ladhu is dancing with a butterfly."

"Butterfly?" asked Garbar. "That ass?"

"Yes. And with Pitki," and off she flew, with the others all rushing helter-skelter after her.

As they got to the back of the hut the strangest sight met their eyes. A lovely blue-and-purple butterfly was flitting up and down, lighting first on Pitki's nose, then on Ladhu's tail, then on Ladhu's ears, then on Pitki's back, then on Ladhu's neck, and so on. And as she went from one to the other, Ladhu hopped and swayed from one leg, to the second, to the third, to the fourth, waggling his head, shaking his ears and turning about. Pitki skipped around him and in between his legs. The butterfly went flit, flit, flit, flit. The sunbeams gleaming on her purple-and-blue wings.

"How on earth, did this begin?" asked Dul Dul, delighted with the fun.

"The butterfly woke up Ladhu by tickling his nose," said Cheep Cheep, "and he began following her. Then Pitki joined in the dance."

"Isn't it grand? Give them a hand," cried Pilla. He sat down and began clap-clap-clapping his paws, adding a nice, jolly "woof" like a bongo drum.

Dul Dul drummed the ground with his hoofs, Garbar rattled his horns, while Cheep Cheep began piping a merry, "Cheep-chirrup! Cheep-chirrup! Cheep-chirrup!"

Suddenly the butterfly flew up and up and away. Straight she went towards the lily pool. Ladhu galloped off after her.

"Come on, Dul Dul," shouted Pilla. "Now is our chance. Fetch the rake. I'll take a bucket. They are headed for the lily pool."

Dul Dul trotted round to Sonoo's hut, picked up the rake and followed him.

"Silly asses! Chumps," muttered Garbar.

"Come on Pitki. Let's join them," said Cheep Cheep.

"First I must nibble some nuts. Oof! I am all puffed and panting," replied Pitki.

"I'll wait for you. But do hurry," added Cheep Cheep.

10

At The Lily Pool

The lilies in the pool were just opening. Some were red and some were purple and some were white. They looked very pretty in the lily pool. The butterfly flew straight to the lilies and went first to a half-opened purple bud. Then she flitted off to a big red bloom. Ladhu galloped along and, much to Dul Dul's surprise and Pilla's relief, just at the edge of the pool, put both front feet forward and stopped dead.

"Second problem solved," said Pilla, only he actually said, "Thecon pwoblem tholbed," because he had the bucket-handles in his mouth and couldn't speak clearly.

"Put the buckets down, Pilla," said Dul Dul when they arrived at the pool, "and help me with the rake."

Dul Dul caught the end of the handle in his mouth, while Pilla took hold of it in the middle. They pushed the rake into the pool. The head sank to the bottom. Then both of them pulled and pulled. The rake had stuck in a big lump of clay. As Dul Dul and Pilla tugged, the clay slowly came away. Then suddenly there was a sloshy gurgle and with a plop, the rake came up with a swing, with the lump of clay stuck to it. Dul Dul and Pilla fell over in a heap.

Ladhu who had been staring at the butterfly now turned and saw them, and he burst out laughing. "Haw! Haw! Hee! Hee!" he roared. "Ho! Hoo! Haw! Hee!" and he rolled about giggling and guffawing.

"Oh, do shut up, Ladhu, and come and help us," snapped Pilla, suddenly very fed up with his crazy friend. "Shut up! Come here!" he shouted.

Ladhu was so shocked at Pilla's shouting at him that he shut up at once and ambled over to where Dul Dul and Pilla lay pinned under the rake.

"Come on now," went on Pilla, "drag the rake off us. It's too heavy for us to move with all that clay stuck to it."

Ladhu took the rake in his mouth and heaved it off. Dul Dul and Pilla scrambled up.

"Thank you, Ladhu," began Dul Dul politely. "That was very clever ..." but before he could finish, Ladhu dropped the rake and burst into tears.

"Hooar! Whoar! Hooar! Hooar!" he bellowed, weeping fit to burst his lungs.

"Oh, dear," said Dul Dul. "Pilla, I am afraid you have hurt his feelings."

11

Garbar Talks Sense

Old Sonoo came out of his hut and saw Garbar all alone. He was spreading out some straw to dry in the sun.

"Where is everyone, Garbar?" he asked.

"Lily pool," was the reply.

"Ah! Yes, of course. What a memory I have. Dul Dul came to take the rake and Pilla ran off with

both buckets. Did I hear some music this morning?" asked Sonoo.

"Music?" scoffed Garbar. "Noise!" he corrected, quite forgetting how much he had enjoyed the funny dance himself.

"Where is Ladhu?" asked Sonoo.

"Ran off," said Garbar with a nod of his head towards the lily pool.

Just then they heard a strange roaring, wailing sound in the distance. It seemed to come from the direction of the pool.

"Goodness. Whatever could that be? Do you think a lion has broken out of the zoo?" quavered Sonoo, in a worried tone.

"Lion? Nonsense! Silly ass, that's who," mumbled Garbar.

"Ladhu?" said Sonoo. "But how can he make such a roaring, awful noise?"

"Ass. That's how," was all Garbar replied.

"Garbar, Garbar," called a high voice from the middle of the tree. Garbar looked up. Mrs Squirrel had poked her head out of her hole.

"Is Pitki with you? What on earth is that rumbling noise? Do you think it is an earthquake?" she asked trembling all over.

"No earthquake. Just the ass" replied Garbar,

"Oh dear! He sounds as if he is in dreadful pain. Good morning Baba*ji*," she added, on seeing Sonoo.

"Good morning, Mrs Squirrel. Don't you worry yourself. I shall go and see what has happened. Garbar would you like to come, too?"

"No. Too much work. Spring-cleaning," replied Garbar, going into the hut.

12

Sonoo Tames The "Lion"

So old Sonoo picked up a stick, just in case he needed it, and hurried off towards the lily pool. As he went along, Sonoo kept thinking and muttering to himself, "Must try and teach Ladhu to be more sensible. He must learn control. But how? And yet, I must say he always seems to do the right thing the wrong way. Dear, dear, what a puzzle it all is."

The noise was louder now and Sonoo could see Ladhu sitting on his haunches with his head up and his ears back and his huge mouth open, bellowing, while tears ran down to form a stream that ran into the lily pool. Pilla was trying to lick him; Dul Dul was trying to talk to him; Cheep Cheep was fluttering above him and Pitki was running round him, but Ladhu was taking no notice of any of them.

"Ho!" shouted Sonoo. "Ho there!" and waving his stick he came running up.

The minute Ladhu heard the shout and saw the waving stick, he shut his mouth, closed his eyes, lay down flat and buried his muzzle between his front legs.

"What does this mean now?" asked Sonoo.

"I think he thinks you are going to beat him with the stick, like his master used to, Babaji," explained Pilla.

Sonoo came up and patted Ladhu.

"Come now, Ladhu," he said gently. "I did not mean to frighten you. Come, sit up. We must take the clay home. You must help us carry it back. You know we can't do anything without your help. You know that. So do get up"

Ladhu raised his head a wee bit. First he opened one eye and then he opened the other. First he raised his forelegs, then he raised his hind legs and finally he stood up, waiting.

"Up with the buckets," cried Pilla, excitedly. Dul Dul and he had already filled them with the clay. The buckets were tied together with rope and Dul Dul slung them across Ladhu's back.

"Come along now," said Sonoo quietly, still patting Ladhu and stroking his ears gently. "Come along, Ladhu. But go slowly my boy because I am old and cannot walk fast."

As obedient as a lamb, Ladhu began ambling back by Sonoo's side. Very quietly all the other friends trooped along behind them.

"Welcome, lion tamer," called Garbar from the hut, as they came up to him. "Food's ready."

The good old goat had done all the housework. There were nuts for Pitki, berries for Cheep Cheep, fruit for Sonoo, a nice big bone for Pilla, fresh hay for Ladhu, which Garbar shared with him. And Dul Dul,

who was a magic clay horse and did not really need any food at all, had a sniff at everybody's fare.

"Oh goody-good. Good old Garbar," cried Pilla, bouncing with joy at the sight of his bone.

"Enough of that," said Garbar gruffly, trying not to show how pleased he was.

Soon all that could be heard was a good munching.

13

The Owl And The Shadows

A bright, full moon shone down on the silent park. A soft breeze was blowing. Among the hanging roots of the banyan, the fire-flies flicked their lights, on-off, on-off, on-off, like so many tiny stars playing hide-and-seek. An owlet gave a low hoot, "Twhoo-whoo-whoo," and from the lily pool the bullfrogs began their gruff serenade.

The little brown owlet flew down from the tree and sat on the roof of the hut beneath, "Twhoo-whoo-whoo," he called. Inside the hut Dul Dul lay fast asleep on his stone slab; Garbar was wheezing a little on his pile of straw and Pilla was dreaming, as usual, of bones and merry chases.

In the hut nearby, old Sonoo lay asleep on his bed, and in the newly built porch of his hut, lay Ladhu, snoring.

"Twhoo-whoo-whoo," called the owlet again.

Nobody answered. The owlet ruffled up his feathers. There was no one to play with and he was feeling lonely. He cocked his head and gave a sharp glance as he saw two shadows move out from under the Big Banyan.

"Twhoo-whoo-whoo are you?" he called softly.

But the shadows went silently by without a sound. They slipped past the hut and slunk softly by the snoring donkey, in the porch of the second hut.

"Twhoo are you?" repeated the owlet, as he flew off to the roof of the second hut. He looked about him, but no shadows moved anywhere.

"They must have gone in," he thought to himself. "I better see what they are up to." He hopped down to the window of Sonoo's hut and peeped in. The potter lay fast asleep, while round his bed two shadows moved about, peering under and sniffing in corners.

"They are up to no good, whoever they are," thought the owlet. "I must give an alarm," and he

flew back on to the roof of the first hut. "Twhoo-whoo-whoo," he called. "Twhoo-whoo-whoo!"

Pilla started out of his dream. "Twhoo-whoo-whoo," he heard the owlet call.

"Drat that silly owl," he muttered. "Doesn't he know it's time to sleep?"

"Twhoo-whoo-whoo," called the owlet.

Pilla bounced up. "I will soon settle him," he thought, and he bounced out of the hut.

"Yap," he barked. "Shut up, silly-billy."

"Twhoo-whoo," cried the owlet, fluttering across to the other hut.

"Twhoo-whoo," he hooted, flying back above Pilla and then back again to Sonoo's window. "Twhoo-whoo."

"Now whatever can be the matter with him?" thought Pilla. "He has got a case of moonlight madness if you ask me," and he ran across to Sonoo's hut.

"Twhoo-look-whoo-you-look-whoo," hooted the owlet.

"Something must be wrong there," thought Pilla, as he bounded across the snoring Ladhu and into the hut. No sooner had he entered than there was a terrific scuffle,

"Mee-ow! Hee-ow! Chee-ow!"

"Piaoo! Niaoo! Chiaoo!"

Screeching and spitting, the two shadowy forms sprang at Pilla.

"Woof! Woof! You nasty things," barked Pilla.

Sonoo woke up with a fright.

"My, my! What on earth is happening?" he cried, as lots of bodies seemed to be flying about his bed.

"Nee-ow! Mee-ow! Chee-ow!"

"Siaoo! Niaoo! Miaoo!"

"Woof! Woof!"

What a noise there was! Ladhu woke up and hearing the din, opened his huge mouth and started singing, "Hee-haw, Hee-haw!" at the top of his voice.

Dul Dul sprang up. "Garbar. Wake up. There is a fight going on in Babaji's hut," and off he went.

"Coming," cried Garbar, as he charged across.

"Twhoo-whoo-whoo," hooted the owlet, enjoying the fun. He didn't feel a bit lonely any more.

Dul Dul and Garbar ran into the hut. Sonoo had just got up and now he lit a small lantern.

In the centre of the room, Pilla was battling furiously with two alley cats. One was a huge marmalade tom with torn ears; the other, a striped, grey, one-eyed fighter.

When the cats saw Garbar and Dul Dul and heard the horrible noise Ladhu was making, they got really scared.

"Mee-ow! Nee-ow!" screeched one.

"Niaoo! Piaoo!" spat the other and off they streaked through the door.

14

Pilla, The Hero

"After them!" cried Pilla.

"No, no, Pilla. Let them go," shouted Sonoo.

The cats whirled past the singing Ladhu with a whining jet whistle, "See-ow!" "Chiaoo!"

The donkey got such a shock that he shut his mouth and stared blankly into the night.

"Dul Dul, catch them!" yapped Pilla, struggling to get away from Sonoo, who was holding on to his wriggling body.

"No, Pilla" said Dul Dul calmly, "Babaji is right. Let them go. You have been very brave, I must say. Are you hurt?"

"Well done, Pilla!" said Garbar.

Pilla was very pleased at being praised by his friends. He stopped wriggling.

"He has scratches all over his face," quavered Sonoo, in a worried voice, "and one of his paws is bleeding."

"Oh, that's nothing," began Pilla grandly.

Then he looked down and saw the little patch of blood.

"Ooo!" he cried, "Ooo, Dul Dul! I'm all trickling away!" and he lay down, with his tail uncurled flat behind him.

"Lick it," ordered Garbar gruffly. Pilla gave a feeble lick at his paw. It tasted salty, but not too bad. He gave another lick.

"Enough!" commanded Garbar.

Sonoo tore a piece of muslin off his scarf and gently wrapped it round the hurt paw.

"Twhoo-whoo," hooted a voice from the window.

"Oh, Dul Dul!" cried Pilla, "we must thank the owlet. It was he who gave us the warning. Do ask him in."

Dul Dul went up to the window. "Thank you, dear owlet. Won't you come in and join us?"

But the light in the room hurt the baby owl's eyes. And he could see a faint ray of light gleaming in the sky. Dawn was about to break and the exciting events of the night had made him quite sleepy. So he shook his head, said a soft "Twhoo-whoo," and off he flew to have a good day's rest.

It was too late to go back to bed, so they all sat round Pilla, while Sonoo dabbed at the scratches on the pup's face with a wet handkerchief. Pilla felt very grand telling them of the night's adventures.

"This was not the first time I have had to fight those nasty, mean things," growled Pilla in a fierce sort of voice. "They both jumped on me near the butcher's shop the other day. They don't fight fair. The cats!" This was about the most horrid name Pilla could think of calling his enemies.

"Won't Cheep Cheep and Pitki be sad at having missed all the excitement," said Dul Dul.

As soon as Ladhu heard Cheep Cheep's and Pitki's names, he got up and dashed off.

"Where's he gone?" asked Garbar,

"I think he wants to fetch our missing friends," said Dul Dul. "Garbar, let's all go. We can carry Pilla."

"Ride," said Garbar to Pilla. The pup understood his shorthand. He tried to get up but his paw felt strange all tied up.

"Wait, Pilla. Let me help you," said Sonoo and he picked up the pup and put him on Garbar's back. They went outside and found Cheep Cheep and Pitki and Mrs Squirrel and Mama Bird, all sitting on a low branch watching Ladhu who was trying to act out Pilla's brave fight with the two cats, in dumb-show. He jabbed a hoof to the right, a hoof to the left, sat back and pummelled the air with both hoofs. He rolled to the left, he rolled to the right, he even turned a somersault. The four friends on the branch stared and stared. Not one of them could guess what he meant by these antics.

Just then Garbar came out with Pilla riding high and Sonoo and Dul Dul, beside them. They all watched Ladhu and the puzzled birds and squirrels. Then Dul Dul gave a laugh and began to sing:

Brave Pilla Pup
Last night got up
To stop an owl from hooting.
'Woof! Woof!' he cried
As the owl he espied,
'Silly bird. You need shooting.'

The Owl flew up
To Sonoo's hut
And kept on 'Too-whoo-whooing.'
'Woof! Woof!' barked the pup,
'Silly Owl, shut up.'
But the Owl would not heed his shooing.

Then Pilla pup
Went dashing up
To see what was the matter.
He had to fight
With all his might
Two cats; one thin; one fatter

At last the watchers understood Ladhu's dumb act. They began clapping with delight as Dul Dul sang on,

Brave Pilla Pup
Deserves a cup
For being such a hero.
So give him a hand
For making his stand
Against the cats without any fear-o.

Pilla got up and made a bow to his cheering friends.

The Tale of
Lumbdoom
the Long-tailed Langur

Dedicated to
Ketan and Vivek

1

The Tale Of Lumbdoom Langur

Great excitement shook the tree tops of Ghanna Jungle! Branches swayed, leaves shivered, birds chirruped, as with a leap and a swing and a chitter-chitter-chatter, dozens and dozens and just dozens of brown, grey, black, yellow and white monkeys hurried along their green highways to the Big Banyan. They were all going to pay a visit to Rani Langur, who had just had twin babies.

Each monkey, big or small, brown or grey, long-tailed, short-tailed or with no tail at all, carried a present. Some brought nuts, some took fruit and some had flowers. But one jolly, brown monkey, with the cheekiest grin you ever saw, carried a large earthen pot! He had snatched it off the head of a frightened village girl near the stream that chuckled merrily over the pebbly slopes of the hill.

Old Raja Langur nodded his head to each new guest as he took the gifts and carefully stored them in a deep hollow in the tree trunk. At last he led the big crowd of monkeys to the place where Rani Langur and the babies lay.

First Raja Langur picked up one of the babies.

"Oh! How pretty!"

"My, she should be called Sundari!"

"Isn't she a pet?" chorused all the Mama and Papa monkeys.

"Sundari she is," announced the Raja, with a gracious nod.

Then he picked up the second little langur. This was a son and the monkeys peered hard at him. But—a gasp went up all around! For, as Raja Langur lifted the little chap higher and higher, they saw that his tail just went on and on and—oh dear!—ON, almost without an end!

Everyone was silent.

Then, with a loud, hoarse cackle the naughty, brown monkey shouted, "Ho! Ho! Ho! Ho! Look

at young long-tail. Why, he's a real 'lumbdoom' langur."

The poor little langur blinked his tiny, black eyes and gave a small, sad sniff at this rude remark.

When the naughty, brown monkey, whose name, funnily enough, was Bhola, which, as you know means "very good" had dubbed the baby langur "Lumbdoom", all the other monkeys were frightened. They were sure Raja Langur would be angry and banish Bhola from Ghanna Jungle. But just then an old, old monkey, the wisest in the clan, came slowly forward. He held up a solemn paw and raised one crooked claw.

"Hush!" murmured the monkeys. "Old Baba Bandar is going to say something."

"This langur is a very special one," quavered Baba
Bandar, in a high, cracked voice. "His tail is a sign of
great powers. He will be able to foretell the future.
Let him be called 'Pandu'!"

"Hail Pandu! Hail Pandu!" chorused the monkey
clan.

The poor little langur blinked his tiny eyes quicker
than before. He did not want to be called "Pandu",
nor did he want to be thought special. But he could
do nothing about it.

All day long, while he watched his sister, Sundari,
playing with the other young langurs and monkeys,
learning to leap and jump and swing he had to sit in
a hollow of the tree trunk. Lots of monkeys came to
see him. They asked him all sorts of silly questions.
The little langur did not answer. He coiled his long

tail round and round in a pile and sat on top of it, with his face sunk into his paws. Sometimes the tip of his tail twitched. Soon all the monkeys took these twitchings to be signs. If his tail moved once they said it meant "Yes", and if it wiggled twice, they felt sure it was "No"!

But the little langur never said a word. He felt too sad and lonely.

2

The Tale Of A Tail

One morning, very early, before Sundari or any of the other monkeys was awake, Lumbdoom, or Pandu as he was now called, crawled out of the hollow in which he was made to spend all his days. He crept slowly along the ground to a clump of young saplings. His long tail dragged behind him and made a rustling noise in the dry leaves. Then it got caught in a fallen log and tripped him up. He fell with quite a thud on his nose.

"Bah! You silly, horrid thing!" whispered Lumbdoom to his tail. "You are always getting me into trouble." He gathered it up, and held on to the tip as he crept on.

When he reached the trees he tried to climb up one that had a low branch, not too far off the ground. First his tail got stuck under a stone, so he had to come down and roll the stone out of the way. Then he began to climb again. This time he almost got up to the branch, but his tail was so heavy, he couldn't keep his balance, and down he came again with a bang!

He sat on the ground, scratching his head, trying to puzzle things out. Suddenly, he had an idea. He rolled his tail into an untidy sort of ball, stood up, holding it carefully in his hands and then, with all his

strength he threw it up towards the low branch. But he did not have the strength to throw it high enough, and as it went up it also pulled him off his hind legs. Plop! He fell on to his face and—whoosh!—his tail fell on top of his head, squashing him underneath!

Lumbdoom crawled out from under the coils of his tail. He was cross! He picked up the tip of that nasty tail and bit it!

"Ouch!" he cried, "that's me!" Well, so it was, and he discovered that that was no way of teaching his tail a lesson! The only thing to do was to try again. So, once more, very, very slowly, inch by inch, Lumbdoom crawled up the tree.

"Oh please, please, please dear tail," he pleaded, "please be good and do not drag me down again!"

At last he was on the branch. How wonderful he felt. He sat on it and pulled his tail up beside him. He felt quite fond of it for a change!

After a short rest, he began to look about for another tree which would be near enough for him to jump to. He saw that the end of the branch he sat upon just touched the leaves of the next tree. He thought that if he could crawl towards the end of the branch he might be able to leap onto the next tree.

When he got to the end of the branch, Lumbdoom leapt up into the air. But as he went up, his tail went

down and, with a sudden spin, Lumbdoom found himself whirling down, down, down, getting all wrapped up in his tail as he went! He landed on the mossy ground looking like a funny sort of cocoon, with his nose and eyes peering out of his tail.

"Ho! Ho! Ho! Ho! Hee! Hee!" cackled a loud, shrill voice and Bhola Bandar came leaping and swinging across to look at Lumbdoom.

"Well! Just look at young long-tail. Perhaps he will soon burst out of his cocoon with wings like a butterfly. Then he'll be able to fly! Ho! Ho! Hee! Hee!"

Lumbdoom almost began to cry, "I th—th—think you are horr-rid," he sniffed. "If y-you w-would only teach m-me how, I could jump and l-leap like y-you."

Bhola, who was really quite a friendly chap and didn't mean to be nasty—he was just thoughtless, like most of us are—felt quite bad. "Why, of course I'll show you how," and he began to jump, leap, swing, turn a double forward somersault, a backward triple handstand and, finally, twirling his tail round a branch, he whirled around like a windmill in a high wind.

"Oh! Please! Stop, stop, stop," cried Lumbdoom, falling back in amazement and covering his eyes, "I'm gid-gid-giddy!"

After a little while, Lumbdoom—who had put his paws over his eyes when Bhola was whirling madly, like a top—peeped through his claws. No one was there! He blinked and blinked.

"Bhola!" he shouted, "please, Bhola, don't run away. Do play with me!"

But all he heard was a crashing in distant branches and a faint "Ho! Ho! Ho!" as Bhola sprang further and further into the green depths of Ghanna Jungle!

Lost and sad, Lumbdoom walked along the ground, holding the tip of his tail. Soon he came to a little stream and there, in the middle of it, sat a busy, wee mouse.

"What are you doing, and who are you?" asked Lumbdoom.

"I am Chooee, the Field Mouse," squeaked the little thing, "and I am washing away the mud from my face."

"Oh! Do you think I could wash away a bit of my tail?" asked Lumbdoom.

"You can try," said Chooee, as she scurried off into the bushes.

Lumbdoom carefully stepped onto a flat stone in the stream. He sat on it, and let his tail down into

the water. It felt cold and a little ticklish! He quite
liked it.

"Ee-ouch!" suddenly Lumbdoom leapt up, pulling
his tail out quickly. There, nipped on to the end of it
was a large blue fish.

Lumbdoom was very cross. He tugged the fish off
and squeezed her.

"Oo-oo! Ee-ee," squealed the poor fish. "P-p-
please, dear f-f-friend, I did- didn't mean ... I thought
it was a-a w-worm." And she began to cry in gasps,
"Oo-ee! I can't br- breathe. Water-w-water!"

Lumbdoom felt sorry for the poor fish, so he threw
her back into the stream. She swam round the stone

and, flicking her tail happily, cried, "Thank you, friend. What is your name?"

"I'm Lumbdoom because I have such a long tail," replied Lumbdoom glumly.

"I think you are very kind, Lumbdoom and I shall never forget you. I'm off to the Big Waters now, but if you ever need my help, ask for Neeli, the Blue Fish," and away she swam.

"Bye-bye, Neeli," said Lumbdoom sadly, waving his tail at her.

Just then he heard a muffled yelp, "Help! Help!"

3

Lumbdoom Makes A Find

"Help!" cried the distant voice, "Help!"

"Where are you?" called Lumbdoom.

"Here."

"Where is 'here'?"

"In a hole by the tree. Oh! Oh! Please help!" Lumbdoom leaped from the stone in the stream onto the bank and hurried round a big tree that stood close by. Between the roots of the tree, which were very large and knotted and grew out of the ground, there was a stone and by the stone was a deep, dark hole.

Lumbdoom crept up to the mouth of the hole and carefully looked in.

"Are you in here?" he called. "I can't see you. Oh! Yes I can!"

For, suddenly, out of the pitch blackness of the hole, shone two, shining green lights.

"Please, dear friend, get me out. The ants down here are horribly rude. They keep biting and won't let me sit — oh! I'm so sore! Please pull me up!"

"However shall I be able to do that?" thought Lumbdoom, who felt very bad for the unknown creature in the pit. He sat by the hole with his chin in his paw and his tail curled up in a pile under him.

Suddenly the tip of his tail gave a twitch. Lumbdoom looked at it and jumped up.

"Why, I have just what you need!" he cried. "Just wait a minute, friend, help is coming."

He turned about and let his tail into the hole. "Hang on to this," he called, "and climb up, while I hold on to a nice, strong root."

Lumbdoom clung to a nearby root with all his strength as he felt something warm and scratchy and heavy take hold of his tail and climb up swiftly. "Hey!" he cried, "go slow, pal, or you'll have me in with you, too!"

"Here I am," said a little voice just behind him.

Lumbdoom turned round and looked into the merry, muddy face of the smallest baby fox you ever saw!

The little fox climbed out of the pit and shook himself all over. He gave a great, big sneeze, "Aa-shoo! Poof, that's better. Thank you, friend. You are a real pal."

"Oh! It was nothing," said Lumbdoom, blushing with pleasure. "It's just lucky I had my tail."

"Your TAIL?" asked the little fox in surprise.

"Yes, you see, I have a lot of tail, that's why I'm called Lumbdoom. I let it into the hole, and you climbed up it. Look how long it is," and Lumbdoom pulled his tail up for the fox to see.

"My, what a lovely tail. How lucky for you, how lucky for me and oh, how funny," said the little fox, getting all mixed up and bursting into giggles.

"What's so funny about it?" grumbled Lumbdoom, who was rather tired of these silly jokes about his tail. He thought that the little fox should be jolly grateful for it, yet here he was laughing just like Bhola.

"Why, I'm not laughing at you! I'm laughing at me," gasped the little fox, whose grammar was not as good as yours and mine! "You will laugh too. Look!" and saying so, the little fox turned his back on Lumbdoom. To his surprise Lumbdoom saw that he had no tail at all!

He gave a gasp, but—politely—did not laugh.

"You see," said the little fox, turning round to look at his bottom, "it is rather odd, isn't it? I have none and you have too much!"

"Never mind," Lumbdoom consoled him, putting his paw on his shoulder, "I have enough for both of us. Let's be friends. Tell me your name."

"Can't you guess it? I'm called Dumkat, of course," replied the little fox. "Ever since I lost it, I mean."

"Lost it? However did you come to do such a thing?"

"Oh that's a long, sad story," said Dumkat.

"Please tell me how it happened, Dumkat," said Lumbdoom. "That is," he added quickly, "if it does not make you too sad to think about it again."

"Oh! It was a dretful speeruns," said the little fox — he loved to use long words without being quite sure how to say them or exactly what they meant — rolling his eyes in a very dramatic manner, "but I don't mind telling you about it, as you just rescued me from a fame worse than death [He meant 'fate']."

The two animals sat down comfortably against the tree roots; Lumbdoom tucked his tail under him, while Dumkat gave a big sigh, made a very solemn face and began the story he was longing to tell.

"My brothers and I live in a lovely big cave in the hill across the stream. Whenever Mama and Papa went out to hunt in the evening, all four of us used to play just outside our home. We never went very far because of — " here Dumkat's voice became a whisper; he looked over his shoulder, first to the left, then to the right and bringing his mouth close to Lumbdoom's ear, he went on, " — do you know of Bhayanak Bheriya, the dratted wolf?"

Lumbdoom's eyes became as round as shiny marbles and he nodded his head, as all forest babies were frightened into shivers at the name of that dreaded jungle prowler.

The little fox went on, "One night while we were playing 'catch-an'-nip', making a lot of noise, we didn't hear old Bhayanak. Suddenly he jumped over a stone. We rushed into our cave, but—" and here the little chap gave a shudder at the memory, "I was last-man-in and—well, you see, that's how I lost it. He gave such a bite—clean off it came—" and Dumkat broke into loud sobs.

"There, there! Don't, please don't cry, Dumkat," said Lumbdoom, putting his arm round his friend and comforting him kindly. "You can share my tail now."

Dumkat soon stopped sobbing and continued his story.

"After that, my naughty brothers would not leave me alone. They teased me, pinched my bobtail, called me 'bunny-rabbit' and changed my name to Dumkat.

I was so fuzzed up, I ran away, and then I fell into that hole."

"One good thing about your being fed up," said Lumbdoom who thought he could teach his new friend to talk properly if he corrected his mistakes without specially pointing them out, but by using the same words again, as though by accident—"is that we have met. I am happy, Dumkat. Promise me that we shall always be together."

"Of course we will. Here's my paw on it," answered the little fox.

"No! No! We must take a solemn vow. Do let's make an 'animal pact'."

An animal pact is a very serious matter. Any two animals who take this vow together must remain good and loyal friends forever; they must help each other in times of danger, even if it means risking their own life and they can never, never break this promise.

"Hooray!" shouted Dumkat turning a somersault, "what fun! I've always wanted to make an animal-pad."

So the two little animals made the vow and this is how they did it. First they brought their faces very close together till the tips of their noses met. Then they took hold of each other's ears with their paws and finally, staring fixedly into each other's eyes, they twisted their heads in opposite directions, up and down, three times to the left, three times to the right. (If you try this out with your best friend you will find that your chum suddenly seems to have only one, enormous eye that stretches right across

the nose and, as you move your head, the eye swings
up and down in the funniest manner!)

   After making the pact, Lumbdoom and Dumkat
set off together.

4

Lumbdoom's Fancy Hat

The two friends walked along, chatting merrily. Lumbdoom's tail kept catching in roots and under stones and tripping him up.

"Whatever shall we do with it?" he asked, as Dumkat helped him up after he had fallen for the sixth time.

"Why not wear it as a pagri round your head? It would make you look very dandified," suggested Dumkat, who meant "dignified".

So Lumbdoom wound his tail round his head in several coils like a Marwari turban-hat. Instead of being impressed by his friend's dignity, Dumkat burst into shouts of laughter, "Ho! Ho! Ho! Hee! Hee! Haw! Haw! Haw—"

But Lumbdoom just smiled and trotted on. He found his new headgear very useful, as it shaded his eyes and kept the sun off his head. Also, it was so nice not to fall on one's face every three or four yards!

So he let Dumkat laugh and laugh till the little fox almost choked on his giggles. He began coughing and spluttering and his tummy ached so much he had to hold on to it with his paws.

"Oh! Oh! Don't make me laugh—oh my—ooh my tum-tum, ooh—" and Dumkat rolled on the ground.

"Here, you silly chap, stop it and get up," said Lumbdoom, patting him hard on his back.

Dumkat sat up and groaned, "Oh, I've laughed too much. Now my tummy feels empty. Do let us find something to eat, Lumbdoom."

The langur looked about him. "Wait! I'll just get you something very nice," he said.

He swiftly climbed up a wild pear tree.

"Here, catch!" he called out, throwing a ripe, yellow pear to Dumkat and burying his own teeth in another juicy one himself.

Dumkat sniffed at the pear Lumbdoom had thrown to him. He wrinkled up his nose, but took a little nibble.

"Pfft!" he spat it out. "Horrid stuff!" he cried, throwing the fruit away.

As the pear rolled into a bush, a frightened bird flew out with a shrill whistle. At the sight of the bird, Dumkat's eyes glistened brightly. He leaped to the bush and before Lumbdoom could swallow a mouthful of pear, Dumkat scooped out two small eggs from a hidden nest, and in one big gulp had swallowed them both. He sat down, licking his chops, smirking happily.

""No! No! Dumkat, you horrid, nasty, wicked—Oh! How could you, Dumkat? You are bad!" cried poor Lumbdoom, who, unable to eat his pear himself, came down and shook his friend by the shoulder. "You must not ...

"Oh bother you!" shouted Dumkat shaking off his hand, "Leave me alone. I shall ..."

"You must not!"

"I will!"

"You won't!"

"I will! I'm not a silly, grass-eating vegetable, like you [he meant 'vegetarian']. I am a strong, brave fox and I shall eat eggs and birds and chicks and ..."

"No! You won't. I shall not let you!" cried Lumbdoom, very angrily.

"I shall, you silly langur!"

"You won't, you horrid butcher!"

"You pumpkin!"

"You monster!"

And, in a trice, their pact of friendship forgotten, the friends began punching and pinching and pummelling each other as hard as they could.

"Awk! Awk! How's that? How's that?" screeched a loud, harsh voice above their heads. "Now then! Now then! Stop it! Stop it!"

The two fighters looked up, startled, and saw on a branch above them a large, bright green and red parrot. He was looking at them very severely.

"What's up? What's up?" he squawked. "What are you fighting over? Tell Miyan Mitthu. I can settle all quarrels. That I can! That I can!" squawked the parrot, swinging on his high perch.

"It's all Dumkat's fault," cried Lumbdoom, "he ate up the poor little birdie's eggs. He's wicked."

"I'm not. Lumbdoom is to blame, Miyan Mitthu," shouted Dumkat. "He wants me to turn into a pumpkin-eating vegetable like him."

"Ho! Ha! Hum! What a silly pair you are," said the parrot, looking at them so severely that they both stood still, eyes on the ground and hands behind their backs.

"I never heard such nonsense. Why? He is a monkey, he must eat fruit and nuts, and he is a fox, so he will eat birds and eggs. And what, pray, is there to fight over in that?" and Miyan Mitthu rocked on his perch, looking wiser than ever.

The friends felt ever so silly. It did sound foolish when put into words.

"Come on now," called the parrot, "shake hands, shake hands."

Lumbdoom turned to Dumkat and Dumkat looked at Lumbdoom and, all of a sudden they both burst out laughing! They shook hands, thumped each other on the back and danced a jig for joy, completely forgetting their quarrel.

They may have gone on giggling and jigging round each other endlessly, but suddenly, Miyan Mitthu gave a piercing scream.

"Watch out! Watch out!" he screeched, "I can see old Bhayanak Bheriya snooping round the bushes. Off with you! Off with—" and not waiting to finish his sentence, the parrot flew away with a great flapping of wings.

5

The Chase

A stunned silence fell upon the forest. Miyan Mitthu had flown away, all the birds seemed to have vanished, and not a bunny or mouse could be seen anywhere.

Lumbdoom and Dumkat froze with fear, but the sudden snapping of a twig warned them of the great danger. They gathered up Lumbdoom's tail and scrambled through a hedge of prickly bushes.

A low growl and a huff-puff noise close by sent them scurrying off again, tripping over tree roots, crawling over big boulders, jumping over ditches and puddles.

But the sound of Bhayanak Bheriya's heavy breathing followed them everywhere. Just then Dumkat spied a hole in a tree; it looked a good place to hide in.

"Hurry, Lumbdoom. Get into—that small—hollow—quick!" he panted between breaths.

Lumbdoom acted quickly. He climbed into the hollow and pulled Dumkat in after him, and they hurriedly hauled up the langur's long tail.

Bhayanak Bheriya gave a loud, wicked, snarly-yarly growl and leaped straight at the hollow.

"Arr — rr, Grr — rr! Godda you fad puddings," he snarled.

Bhayanak Bheriya always had a horrid cold and never could say his "t's" and "n's" clearly. In fact, you could barely understand what he was saying, but since he never said anything very pleasant it did not really matter.

"Ooh!" squealed Dumkat, crouched inside the hollow, "now that dratted wolf has got us!"

As Bhayanak Bheriya leapt at the hollow where Lumbdoom and Dumkat crouched in terror, fearing their end had come, the oddest thing happened. The great wolf had heaved himself up with such force that his head and neck shot straight into the opening, but it was too narrow for the rest of him. So, there he hung, with his head stuck inside and his body wriggling outside! He clawed and scratched and

turned and twisted, but try as he might he could not push in any further.

Inside the tree trunk the two friends crouched just out of reach of the snapping jaws of their foe.

"Gr-rr-rr jusd you waid," snuffled the horrid wolf, "I'll get you fellows! Thad I will. Grr-rr!" and he wriggled more than ever, with his tongue hanging out.

Lumbdoom and Dumkat stared wide-eyed, held their breath and watched. Then Dumkat, who could never keep still for long and was always busy thinking up some mischief, had a bright idea. He was still very cross with Bhayanak Bheriya for having bitten off his tail, so now, seeing his hated enemy in a fix, he wanted to have his own back on him.

Picking up the tip of Lumbdoom's tail he began tickling the wolf with it, teasing and taunting him.

"Hee! Hee! Ho! Ho!" he chortled as the wolf tried to avoid the tickly, fuzzy tail-end, "take that, you nasty old hydrant [he meant 'tyrant'!]!" And he patted Bhayanak Bheriya's nose as with a powder puff, while poor Lumbdoom, whose teeth were chattering with fear, tried to hold him back.

"Aa—as—as-tish-sh-oo!" sneezed the wolf, with such a mighty push of his front paws against the tree trunk that his head gave a loud "pop" as it burst from the hole like a cork from a bottle, and he fell back on the ground, rolled over and over and landed in a bush full of prickles.

Dumkat peered out of the hollow, with Lumbdoom peeping over his shoulder, and both of them burst into cheers and giggles as they saw Bhayanak Bheriya scramble to his feet and run, howling with pain, into the jungle, with his tail between his legs.

Thrilled by their victory over the nasty wolf, Lumbdoom and Dumkat gave three loud cheers, patted each other on the back and curling up together at the bottom of the hollow, fell asleep.

Suddenly Lumbdoom felt someone give him a push. "Go to sleep, Dumkat," he mumbled, sleepily, "don't push me."

There was no reply. Again he felt he was being given a shove from behind. He sat up; rubbed his eyes and looked at Dumkat. The little fox was fast asleep. Lumbdoom couldn't doubt that when Dumkat gave a wheezy sort of snore!

Turning around, the langur tried to go to sleep again.

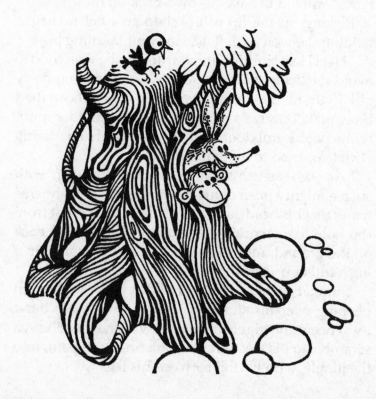

"Perhaps I am just imagining things," he thought, as he settled down once more.

But before he could properly shut his eyes he was pushed so violently that he rolled right over. "I can't be dreaming," he thought, very puzzled indeed. "I am certain something very odd is happening."

He looked round the hollow, up into the dark trunk. No sign of any living creature could be seen, and Dumkat was still blissfully asleep.

Then as Lumbdoom gazed at his sleeping friend, he saw Dumkat being slowly rocked from side to side.

"Good heavens! Is it an earthquake?" thought the langur, who had never been in one himself, but had heard his elders talk about them.

He peered closely at the fox, then drew back in horror! His hair stood up on end, his eyes grew wide, his teeth chattered.

Putting out a trembling paw he shook Dumkat.

"Oh wake up, Dumkat, please wake up!" he whispered. "Don't make a noise but please wake up," he went on, as the fox stirred and opened his eyes.

"What's it now?" asked Dumkat, rather cross at being disturbed.

"W—we w-will have to st-steal out c-carefully," whispered Lumbdoom, hurriedly, trying to stop his teeth from chattering with fear.

"Why, you ninny? Aren't you comfy? This is the luxuriest bed I've had for ages," replied Dumkat.

"Oh, oh! No, no! Dumkat, come away," urged Lumbdoom. "This comfy bed of ours is no luxury— it's really Ajgar the Python. And he is just waking

up from his sleep. Hurry, hurry! And don't make a noise," he added as Dumkat's hackles rose with fear and his eyes almost popped out of his head.

Slowly and very quietly Lumbdoom and Dumkat began creeping towards the opening of the hollow. Old Ajgar the Python, helped them on by giving a sudden heave. They rolled over and bumped their heads sharply together.

"Ouch!" cried the langur.

"Eeawk!" yelped the little fox.

Ajgar gave a sharp hiss, unwinding slowly. He was heavy with sleep and although he was cross about having his hidden bedroom invaded by two cheeky youngsters, he was also quite hungry. He had been asleep for some days, digesting his last large meal. It was about time for him to fill up again, before falling off into a satisfied slumber once more.

Lumbdoom and Dumkat did not wait to wish him good evening or a hearty appetite for dinner. They knew that once Ajgar was fully awake he could travel at a very swift speed, gliding over every obstacle that came in the way. Dumkat leapt from the hollow and Lumbdoom climbed down, not forgetting his tail behind him. There was no time to twine it elegantly into a turban as before. So he just wrapped it round his waist like a cummerbund.

Not daring to look behind to see whether they were being followed, the two little animals ran and ran, through the evening dusk, till they came to a river. Panting for breath, they looked about for a means of crossing it.

"Dumkat," whispered Lumbdoom, timidly peeping over his shoulder, "I don't think Ajgar is following us at all."

Dumkat flopped down on the grassy bank thankfully.

"Good! I wish I'd known that sooner, I'm so tired and sleepy."

"Look!" said Lumbdoom pointing to a little boat that was tied to a tree on the bank of the river.

"The very thing!" cried Dumkat scrambling up and tottering off to the boat.

"Come on, Lumbdoom," he went on clambering in and curling up on the bottom, "this is as good as a rocking bed!"

Lumbdoom got in, too, with a sigh of happiness. He lay down next to his friend and soon both of them were fast asleep, pillowed on Lumbdoom's tail which was piled into a cushion under their heads.

6

A Mischievous Wild Wind

All through the night the little boat rocked gently on the water and the two tired animals lay fast asleep. But just as dawn was breaking and the sun slowly rose over the green hills, and the first daring, dancing rays found their way through the tall jungle trees—a breeze sprang up.

It was, at first, just a gentle, teasing breeze. It tumbled the waves over one another and made the boat rock like a hammock; it ruffled the fur of the sleepers and tickled them behind the ears. Then it grew bolder and wilder—rustling through the leafy trees with a great bustling and whistling in the hollows—and feeling very pleased with its antics, it puffed itself up like a great, big bully and became both rude and rough. It tore the little bushes up by their roots and brought down a slender sapling. It knocked a bird's nest out of a tree and scattered the sleepy occupants into a puddle; it tugged and tugged at the rope that bound the little boat to the tree and finally—with a sudden gust—snapped the rope in two and twirling the boat on an eddy, blew it along, down the stream. The waves billowed and heaved, and tumbled and tossed over one another, quite unable to resist the bullying breeze which had, by now, grown into a whirling high wind.

Lumbdoom and Dumkat slept on, unaware of their plight. Dumkat was in the middle of a happy dream and he wriggled with pleasure and gave a little yelp of delight, but he still did not wake up.

Suddenly a shriek pierced through the howling wind.

"Wake up! Wake up! Too late! Too late! Dumkat, Lumbdoom! Wake up! The fall—the waterfall!" and old Miyan Mitthu battling against the wind, flew over the boat, and dive-bombed at the sleepers, screaming shrilly, "Wake up, sillies!' You silly-billy monkey—Lumbdoom—" and he swooped over the friends. But the wind pulled him up and away with it, towards the other shore.

"Dumkat! Lumbdoom!" he called again.

"Hullo! What is it?" mumbled Lumbdoom sleepily.

"Wake up!" came a faint cry. "The waterfall—Lumb—doo—oom."

"Fall? What fall?—Oh! Dumkat, Dumkat! Wake up," cried Lumbdoom, wide awake and fully aware of the terrible danger. He shook Dumkat, holding on to the rocking boat with one paw.

"What is it?" gasped the little fox, sitting up and staring about him, wildly.

"Oh! Oh! The fall—Dumkat, we are heading for the waterfall! Whatever shall we do?"

The little friends clung to each other, as the boat danced and whirled and twirled and tossed, on and on, towards the dreaded waterfall. Bobbing up and down like a cork, the small boat sailed on and on; Lumbdoom and Dumkat clung to the edge to keep themselves from being tossed overboard. The roar of the waterfall rose above the howling of the wild wind. They stared at each other in dismay.

Lumbdoom looked about him, searching frantically for some sign of hope. He clutched Dumkat's shoulder and shouted through the noise of wind and water, "Dumkat! Look!"

Dumkat turned carefully. He saw the branch of a tree leaning over the stream almost touching the water. The tree stood on the bank, just a few yards above the point where the stream suddenly plunged down a steep fall, over twenty feet, into a whirlpool below.

Gritting his teeth, Lumbdoom moved over to the edge of the boat.

In the meantime, Miyan Mitthu had flown across the jungle, shrieking his dreaded message of disaster on the stream to all the jungle folk. Lots of little creatures, field mice and rabbits, monkeys and langurs, an otter and a mongoose, hurried to the bank to see if they could help the animals in distress. Shakily Lumbdoom stood up in the boat.

"Watch out!" yelled Dumkat, holding out his paws to steady his friend.

As the boat went under the low, hanging branch, the langur threw his tail up like a lasso, winding it around the branch, and grabbing Dumkat by the paws, he squeaked, "Hang on, Dumkat. Don't let go. Hang on to me!"

Dumkat gritted his teeth and clinging on to Lumbdoom raised his hind legs as high as he could. The boat swept on with the current, leaving the two chums dangling on the branch. It dashed against a rock and then plunged down, down, down, whirling madly like a top. It sank into the whirlpool below, and was lost forever.

"Oh!" gasped Dumkat closing his eyes. I'm growing dizzy."

"Don't let — go!" cried Lumbdoom, whose tail was aching with the strain.

Just then they heard a loud cackling laugh in the tree above them.

"Ho ho, hee hee, haw haw! Well, well! Look who's here? Our young friend the long-tailed langur!" and Bhola Bandar peered down at the pair below him. "Hold on, chums," he called, "we'll soon pull you up."

Bhola Bandar climbed to the end of the branch, where Lumbdoom's tail twitched and itched with the ache of clinging round it. He lay along the branch and reaching down, caught Lumbdoom by his hind legs.

"Come on, pals," he called over his shoulder,"come and lend a paw, all of you!"

In a flash there was a great scurry of feet and rustling of leaves, as lots of little creatures scrambled up the tree. First came three young tree cats. They edged up to Bhola Bandar, one behind the other. The first one caught Bhola Bandar's tail. The second hung on to the first cat's tail, the third to the second's.

Then came two monkeys, and they extended the chain in the same way. Behind them were four langurs, and the last one's tail hung down almost to the ground. So a bunny took hold of it. A wild hare caught the bunny's little bobtail. Chattering with excitement and very ready to help, six little field mice formed a chain as well, their leader clinging on to the hare's short stump.

"Now then," called Bhola Bandar. "Ready? One— two— three—HEAVE!"

They all gave a mighty tug and—CR—RA—CK! Down came the branch! But, thank goodness, it swung inwards towards the bank. All the animals

fell with a squeak and a squeal, and only Dumkat at the very end, got a ducking in the stream.

"Ho! Ho!" chortled the brown monkey, "what a fine show!"

He got up and quickly pulled Dumkat out of the water, on to the bank, where all the animals stood around Lumbdoom.

"Hooray!" they cried, as the little fox joined the crowd, and Bhola Bandar thumped him on the back to make him spit out the water he had swallowed.

"I'm s—s—so c—c—cold," shivered Dumkat.

"If you're feeling cold, you'd better jump about a bit," advised Bhola Bandar, thumping Dumkat on the back.

"Here! Wait! I've got it!" cried one of the little tree cats, spying Lumbdoom's tail lying on the ground. He picked up the end of it and began swinging it round like a skipping rope.

"Come on, Dumkat," he cried, "leap in. We'll all sing for you."

And he began to chant, "Teddy bear, Teddy bear, touch the ground ..."

"Yes! Yes! Let's skip," cried the other cats. Dumkat jumped in first and the cats joined in.

"Teddy bear, Teddy bear, turn around ..." You know how it goes. Soon everybody stood about them clapping and singing while Lumbdoom laughed and laughed.

"Careful! Careful!" screeched a warning voice.

A sudden hush fell on the group of happy animals. The wind had died down and not a leaf rustled. They all looked up. Old Miyan Mitthu circled around them twice, and then perched on a branch overhead.

"That's enough. That's enough," he squawked. "Playtime is over. You must think. Think of a way. Think of a way," he went on in his repetitious, fussy manner.

"Think of what?" asked Lumbdoom.

All the creatures gathered about the tree. Some of the langurs and monkeys climbed up the trunk.

Miyan Mitthu looked at them, nodded his head; blinked an eye; raised a claw and spoke slowly, "Got to act. Only way out. Only way out."

"Out where? Act how?" asked Dumkat, getting somewhat muddled. "Why are you so selective?"

"He means secretive," Lumbdoom put in quickly.

"That's what I said," Dumkat spoke rather gruffly.

"Listen well, listen well," said the parrot. "The time has come for all of us to do something about our enemies. You know who — the big, bad two."

"Who?"

"Two. Two."

"Two who?"

"Shoo!" cried all the animals, trying to hush Dumkat, who was asking such questions.

Lumbdoom nudged his friend and he whispered, "I think he means Bhayanak Bheriya and Ajgar the Python."

"That's who! Those two," said the parrot, who had very sharp ears. "About time. Think, my friends. Think hard."

All the little animals looked at each other and tried not to shiver and shake. They all began to think very hard.

7

Of Plots And Plans

They all sat around old Miyan Mitthu, thinking and thinking. They were trying hard to work out a plan by which they could get rid of their enemies, Ajgar the Python and Bhayanak Bheriya.

"I scratched out their eyes with my claws!" cried a small, fierce tree cat.

"Ho! Ho! They'll gobble you up before you can say mee-ow," laughed Bhola Bandar.

"Can't we run away to another wood?" timidly asked Hiranakshi, the gentle deer.

"They would follow us," replied Bhola Bandar. "Or we might find leopards ..."

"... and panthers," put in Lumbdoom.

"Or weasels ..." gasped a bunny.

"... and stoats or hyenas," added the hare.

"Oh! Oh! Whatever can we do?" cried Hiranakshi.

"Let's surround them," began Lumbdoom.

"Yes, yes!" cried Dumkat, "we can capture them, if we all pounce together and then we can ..."

"Pinch them!"

"Pummel them!"

"Stamp on them!'

"Strangle them!"

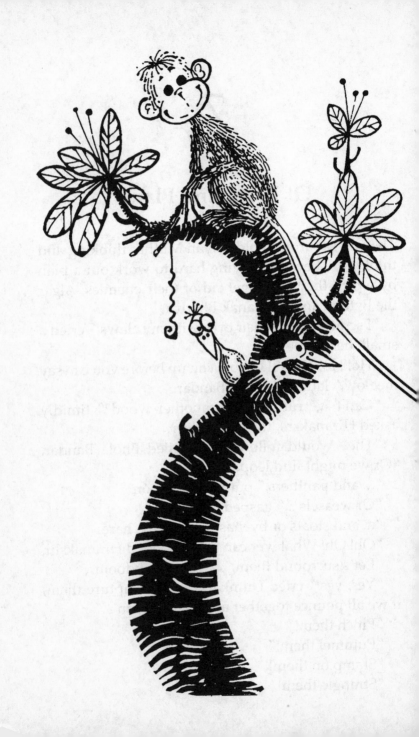

Shouting and screaming out their suggestions, all the little folk began jumping about in a frenzy, as though they were actually finishing off their foes.

"Quiet! Quiet! Order!" squawked Miyan Mitthu. "Silly ones. Stupid ones," he scolded.

The animals were silent, they sat down quietly, feeling rather foolish.

"Now listen to me," went on the parrot, "this is what we must do."

"Draw nearer, Dumkat, and you too, Lumbdoom. For our plot will depend on you two, though all of us must help."

They all drew close together and listened very carefully. Then Miyan Mitthu told the woodland folk of a wonderful way to rid the forest of Bhayanak Bheriya and Ajgar the Python. All the little animals were very excited and they began to prepare for the day they could carry out his excellent plan.

"Come on, Dumkat," said Lumbdoom, "you and I will have to work very hard."

"Oh dear," sighed the little fox, "I am feeling too extorted to move."

"Really, Dumkat, if you mean 'exhausted' why don't you say so. In any case, I've no time to waste on you," went on the langur, "if you are so tired, go to sleep and I shall ask one of the tree cats to do the lasso trick with me. Of course, it's the most important part of our plot, and we must be expert at it."

"No, no, Lumbdoom! Don't you dare ask the cats. You know only I could be dazzling enough to..."

Here Lumbdoom burst out laughing.

"Dazzling, oh my! Oh my!" he spluttered, "just look at the bright, dazzling dare-devil!" And for once, the little langur enjoyed himself hugely at his friend's expense. Dumkat sulked and frowned. But he could not be cross for long and he knew he often mixed up big words and got them all wrong. He soon joined in the laugh against himself.

"You know what I mean, old pal," he chuckled merrily, "so let's get cracking."

Lumbdoom sat on a tree and began casting his tail like a lasso, whipping the end round Dumkat and pulling him up. Sometimes the little fox sat in a ditch while the langur perched on a rock. At other times, Dumkat hid in a deep hole, and Lumbdoom practised rescuing him from there.

Day after day, the two chums kept up their tricks, till finally, Lumbdoom did not need to throw his long tail. He had learnt to whip it out on its own like a spring cord, to coil it round Dumkat and to reel him in like a fish on an automatic rod-and-line.

Now all was ready for the surprise attack!

8

Dumkat Risks His Life

Very early next morning, before the first little chick-a-dee had chirruped the forest folk awake, while the wood was still dark with the shadows of the night and the dew sparkled in the grass, as though the sky had tossed handfuls of shiny stars, Dumkat shook Lumbdoom and whispered in his ear, "Wake up, lazy bones! Don't you know what day this is? We have to be off before sun is up."

"Just one more snooze," pleaded Lumbdoom, in a mumble, turning over onto the other side.

There was a rustling of leaves outside the little hollow where the pals slept. And a moment later Miyan Mitthu peered into the hole and said in as soft a voice as he could manage, "Wake up! Hurry up! We are all set and ready. Waiting for you. Waiting for you."

At his repeated calls Lumbdoom scrambled up at once, and both the little animals set off together. "Good luck to you," called the parrot.

"And to all of you, too," shouted back the chums.

"Don't forget, be brave and all will be well," Miyan Mitthu replied, flying off with a flap of the wings.

The little fox and the langur halted at the foot of a tree. It grew in a turny-twisty way with a low branch hanging over an old dry well. Very solemnly Lumbdoom and Dumkat shook hands and repeated once more the vow of the "animal pact" that made them friends forever.

"Be careful, Dumkat. Don't take more of a risk than you need to."

"I'll be scrumptiously careful," said the little fox, meaning scrupulously, but with such a wise look that Lumbdoom did not dare laugh or try to correct him! "All will be fine if Miyan Mitthu and Bhola don't let us down."

"They won't," assured Lumbdoom, climbing up the tree and lying along the overhanging branch.

Dumkat trotted off. He went straight to Ajgar's hide-out. The huge snake was sleeping. Dumkat nipped his tail sharply. As the reptile un-coiled and saw him, the little fox again bit him. In a flash, Dumkat ran off with the python in pursuit.

Lumbdoom laid waiting on the branch. Suddenly he heard a rumbling to his right. Far in the distance he could see a cloud of dust approaching rapidly. Good old Miyan Mitthu was doing his bit well. But where was Dumkat?

With a hiss and a rustle and a flash and a dart, two forms dashed out from a bush to his left. The first was Dumkat, who ran straight for the old well and, without a pause, jumped in. Quickly as a shooting jet Ajgar followed.

While Dumkat was keeping Ajgar busy and Lumbdoom was sitting watchfully on the tree by the well, old Miyan Mitthu had not been lagging behind. His part of the big attack was to deal with Bhayanak Bheriya.

First the parrot woke up Bhola Bandar. "Come on, Bhola, round up your boys," he told him.

"We'll be there, armed with thorny whips and lots of 'ammunition', too" laughed Bhola Bandar. "We have spent all these days storing up hard raw *ambi*s and, by Jove, they are tough little bullets."

Chuckling to himself, Bhola Bandar gave a call and suddenly the whole jungle seemed alive and crawling, as scores and scores and just scores of monkeys crept, swung and climbed up after their brown chief. They all carried sticks, stones, and raw mangoes.

Soon Miyan Mitthu joined them with dozens of tree cats, rabbits, hares and mice.

In wave upon wave of dark, slinking shadows, the steady stream of animals poured down a glade to the wolf's den. Bhayanak Bheriya was sleeping peacefully.

Bhola Bandar held up a paw. "Remember, all of you, at the signal let it sing," he whispered. The animals nodded.

"Now then, one, two, three, altogether: ROAR!"
"WHAAOO-WRROO-YA A-OO-HOOP!"

The shout rang through the forest like a clap of rolling thunder! Bhayanak Bheriya woke with a yelp of fear. Around him it seemed as though all the devils and demons of the jungle were holding a war dance. With his tail between his legs, he bolted.

The whole whooping crowd swarmed after the harried creature and, with Miyan Mitthu to pilot them, they led the wolf straight towards the old well where Lumbdoom waited.

Panting and puffing, Bhayanak Bheriya ran for his life, not daring to glance over his shoulder to look at the creatures that were pursuing him. He was certain they were the devils of the jungle who were said to haunt the Bhooth Goofa (Ghost's Cave) under the big rock on the other side of the green hill.

Bhayanak Bheriya had often heard his father tell him a terrible tale—when he was just a wolf cub—about it. On a dark and dreadful night, a storm had arisen. Thunder shook the mountains and lightning struck the top-most deodars on the green hill. A forest fire spread wildly, the flames streaking out from tree to tree. In their panic, many of the animals had run down towards the stream, but some, losing their sense of direction, had tried to escape the fire by running round the green hill.

Once there, they had nowhere to hide but in the cave beneath a rocky crag. Here they had crouched, howling in fear and pain. But they had not escaped the roaring flames, for the fire swept past the cave and licked along the pine-needle strewn ground right into the far end of the cavern. Each one of the creatures trapped in there had died and ever since, it was said, their ghosts haunted the forest.

So Bhayanak Bheriya ran and ran and ran. Every time he tried to duck behind a bush, or hide in a ditch, old Miyan Mitthu, screeching in a high and grating voice, would swoop down and peck him hard on the head. Bhayanak Bheriya would shoot off again.

Lumbdoom sat perched in readiness on the tree. He heard the loud whooping of the animals and saw Bhayanak Bheriya heading towards the well.

Just then Dumkat flashed beneath the tree and leaped into the well. Ajgar glided like a streak of lightning after him. Before the end of the long snake disappeared from sight, Bhayanak Bheriya came rushing along and, seeing no other means of escape, he too jumped into the well and vanished.

9

Looping The Loop

When Dumkat had so bravely leaped into the deep, dark, dry well, without so much as batting an eye, he knew exactly what he was up to. Week after week Lumbdoom and he had been hard at work, practising a very difficult and daring turn that would have done credit to an old circus hand!

Half-way down the old well there was a break in the smooth rounded wall. Here a family of rats had lived for many years, having carefully hollowed out a large roomy home. But disaster had struck the poor rat family. A very large, hooting, Horned Owl had discovered their hide-out and had eaten up all the rats that lived there.

Dumkat had learnt to jump in such an expert manner from the opposite side of the well, that he landed on the edge of this deserted hollow. By clinging on and wedging himself in, he could just manage to fit inside it, with half his body sticking out. Lumbdoom would wait till Dumkat had jumped into the well, count three slowly and then shoot his tail down and loop it round Dumkat. Then with a swoosh and a swirl he would yank him out and up on to the tree beside him.

This wonderful, acrobatic trick had not been easy, you can be sure. Over and over again Dumkat had struck against the wall, too high or too low, and had fallen down to the bottom. Lumbdoom had had to pull him up with his tail "lasso" many a time. Or, even if Dumkat made a perfect jump, the langur's tail would shoot out at a wrong angle and it would take ages for Lumbdoom to learn to "loop

the loop" correctly. Time was very short. He had to be able to pull Dumkat out before the count of ten was over.

Dumkat jumped perfectly on the great day. Ajgar glided down the well, straight to the bottom. Before

he could get there a great, shaggy form hurtled past him. It was Bhayanak Bheriya.

Without losing another second Lumbdoom shot out his tail and before you could blink your eye, there was Dumkat being whirled up in the air and safely landed on the tree beside his pal.

While Dumkat was being whirled up to safety by his chum, the langur, a strange and dreadful drama was taking place at the bottom of the well. Two wild and fierce jungle creatures were joined in a life-and-death-struggle — a fight to the finish.

Bhayanak Bheriya had scarcely fallen on to the stony bottom of the well when the python, hissing in fury, was upon him. Baring his long, yellow fangs, his hackles rising in anger and fear, the wolf uttered fierce growls of rage and sprang upon the snake. He sank his teeth into the python just below the hood. Ajgar shuddered, but his heavy, shiny body wriggled in long ripples, as he slowly coiled himself about the wolf.

Feeling those deadly coils round him, Bhayanak Bheriya's growls turned to savage howls. He now tried to disentangle himself, but, unable to do so, made a more ferocious attack — this time going straight for Ajgar's beady eyes.

To and fro the battling enemies thrashed about at the bottom of the well, their bodies striking against its sides and floor. Howls and hisses intermingled.

Over the edge of the well dozens of small faces peered, as all the little folk of the jungle crouched round the top of the battle-field. They uttered no sound; they held their breath; their eyes were full of fear.

Then a sudden shudder ran through the watching animals as with a final howl and hiss of pain the battle ended. Nothing moved. Not a sound was heard. It was over. Both the dreaded enemies were dead.

10

A Song Of Triumph

For a while all was quiet. It was as though the whole jungle held its breath—waiting—unable to believe that the two evil hunters were dead. But both Ajgar and Bhayanak Bheriya lay still. They were indeed lifeless. Never again would the trees shake and shiver at the desperate cries of a little rabbit or a pheasant as Bhayanak Bheriya snarled and snapped them up. Never again would the very grass stand still with horror as the terrible python caught the timid deer or little fox in its coils and swallowed it. The tyrants were well and truly dead.

"Ho! Ho! Ho! Hee! Hee! Haw Haw!"

It was Bhola Bandar, of course, who broke the silence, with a wild guffaw of joy. Once the spell was broken all the little folk began laughing and cheering and whooping with delight. They slapped each other on the back, danced funny little jigs, leaped over each other and finally they lifted Dumkat and Lumbdoom on to their shoulders and "chaired" them with much clapping and cheering.

Dumkat greeted the cheers with the fighters' salute, while Lumbdoom looked like a king, waving his hand, his long tail being carried like a royal train by all the tiny mice!

Then led by Bhola Bandar, all the little folk burst into a gay song, banging on stones with sticks as they sang it. And this is what they sang:

> *Dumta Dumtee*
> *Way! Woo! Wah!*
> *Ring the 'ghunti'*
> *Where e'er you are!*
> *Ajgar, the slimy,*
> *Bhayanak, the sly,*
> *Horrid old meanies,*
> *Both had to die.*
>
> *So our heroes*
> *Monkey and fox,*
> *Caught both big foes*
> *As tho' in a box.*
>
> *Into the dry well*
> *Jumped brave Dumkat*
> *After him Ajgar went*
> *The silly mutt!*
>
> *Chasing the Bheriya*
> *Came the small folk.*
> *He followed the python.*
> *Oh! What a joke!*
>
> *Dumtee Dumta*
> *Wah! Way! Woo!*
> *Strike the 'ghunta'*
> *And all shout 'Boo'!*

Throwing his lasso
With much care
Lumbdoom whirled Dumkat
Up in the air.

Ajgar gave Bhayanak
Such a fond squeeze,
He forced the old wolf
Onto his knees.

Bhayanak bit Ajgar
With all his might
The little folk shuddered
As they watched the fight.

Bhayanak and Ajgar
Are now both dead.
And all the little folk
Can live without dread.

Dumta Dumtoo
Woo! Wah! Way!
Beat the 'dumeroo'
Let's all be gay!

Shouting "Wah! Wah! Woo! Woo!" they came to a little glen where a whole crowd of jungle folk were waiting for them.

11

An End And A Beginning

Ghanna Jungle wore a festive air. All the trees put out their freshest leaves, faintly tinted with pink and yellow. Every bush wore a garland of bright butterflies that fluttered and rested, and rested and fluttered in changing patterns, over each shrub and blossom. White and mauve violets snuggled cosily between cushions of the greenest moss, pink and red *jabakusum* shook their merry bell-like heads in the gentle breeze and the long, graceful tendrils of *amaltash* tossed and glinted like pure gold in the gleaming sunlight.

All the mamas and papas and grannies and grandpas and uncles and aunts and cousins and friends of the brave band of little folk who had ganged up together, under the wise leadership of Miyan Mitthu, to rid the jungle of Ajgar and Bhayanak Bheriya, were gathered in the glen to welcome them back.

Old Raja Langur, who was Lumbdoom's father, with Rani Langur and his sister Sundari were beaming with pride and delight, as they saw Lumbdoom being carried in triumph by his friends.

Dumkat's naughty, teasing brothers and sisters were staring and staring, with their round eyes almost popping out of their heads in disbelief, at the sight of Dumkat, high up on a tree cat's shoulders, waving his fists like a champion prizefighter. They felt so ashamed of their rudeness and cruelty to their brave brother, who had helped to get rid of the horrid wolf who had snapped off his pretty tail.

Oh! What a burst of cheering and clapping and hugging and kissing greeted the band of heroes! For a while all Ghanna Jungle echoed and reechoed to the sound of the laughter and cheers of the

little folk, and the ground actually shook with the jumping and stamping and dancing and leaping of all the merry-makers.

"Now then! Now then! That's enough! Quite enough!" It was old Miyan Mitthu who sat on a branch out of harm's way — for he was most alarmed by all the paws and claws that were being waved around in such a wild manner — who called them all to order.

"Yes yes, indeed," said Raja Langur, in a loud, deep voice. "We must now proceed with method. What shall come first, my dear?" asked he, turning to Rani Langur.

"First the feast," replied the Rani Langur.

At this there was another round of cheers, as all the animals trooped off to a dell where the choicest spread of food met their eyes! Fruits of every kind, oranges, apricots, bananas, *sitaphal*, *papita*, mangoes, *jamuns*, *beyrs*, pomegranates and guavas—oh, how their mouths watered as they sat down to eat them! There were almonds and walnuts and peanuts and coconuts—what a lot of cracking and crunching began!

After the feast the youngsters could no longer sit still. Bhola Bandar called out, "Sit down all mamas and papas and now we youngsters will entertain you!"

Then began the grandest show you can imagine! It was better than the best circus turns you ever

saw. Lumbdoom did his lassoing trick, Dumkat leaped and turned in the air like a trapeze acrobat and Bhola Bander whirled like a spinning top from a slender branch.

The very old and very young animals sat and watched, enthralled! Miyan Mitthu perched on a tree and gave a most wise and witty running commentary on each event.

When it was over and dusk began to fall, Raja Langur asked his son, "Well, Lumbdoom, will you return home with us?"

The fox family turned to Dumkat and said, "We must take you back to the den."

But the chums stood together and looked at their families and shook their heads.

"No thank you, Papa," said Lumbdoom. "I have to leave Ghanna Jungle for I have a lot to see and learn."

"No thanks, dear brothers and sisters," added Dumkat, "I'm off to the wide, wide world with my chum, Lumbdoom. We are going to be fabulous exploders."

"He means famous explorers," put in Lumbdoom quickly, nudging his pal in the ribs.

"That's what I said," chipped in the fox, "we'll be the most fastidious exploiters you ever heard of!"

"Shut up, you chump!" whispered Lumbdoom fiercely, "and come along."

And so, paw in paw, and with big grins wreathing their faces, Lumbdoom, the long-tailed langur and Dumkat, the tailless fox, waved goodbye to their families and friends and left Ghanna Jungle, to meet all the adventures they could find in the beautiful, big world beyond.

UMA ANAND was born in the year 1923 in Lahore, Pakistan. She was wife of the prominent Bollywood film director Chetan Anand and mother of Ketan Anand and Vivek Anand.

Uma Anand was a well-known journalist and children's author. Several of her children's books were translated and published into various Indian languages. For many years she wrote as Aunty Wendy in the *Illustrated Weekly of India* and also conducted the Children's Hour programme in New Delhi and Mumbai over All India Radio. She was the editor of *Sangeet Natak*—a journal on the performing arts published by the Sangeet Natak Akademi. Uma Anand died on 13 November 2009.

MARIO MIRANDA was born on 2 May 1926 in Daman. He was one of India's most versatile illustrators. In 1953, he began his career as a Cartoonist for the Times of India Group. He had illustrated numerous books. Mario Miranda was the recipient of many national and international honours. He died on 11 December 2011 in his ancestral house in Goa.